THE POET ASSASSINATED

AND OTHER STORIES

BY GUILLAUME APOLLINAIRE

TRANSLATED FROM THE FRENCH

BY RON PADGETT

NORTH POINT PRESS SAN FRANCISCO 1984

(*Le Poète assassiné* originally published 1916
by the Bibliothèque des Curieux)
Printed in the United States of America
Library of Congress Catalogue Card Number: 83-063131
ISBN: 0-86547-151-7

This translation is dedicated to the memory of Ted Berrigan.

TABLE OF CONTENTS

ACKNOWLEDGMENTS

As a poet who translates for the pleasure of it, and not a scholar, I would have been lost without the help of many friends and colleagues in the preparation of this translation.

It was Kenneth Koch's advice on translating and his inspiring enthusiasm for Apollinaire that led me to this project.

Gratitude is due to those who helped with the 1968 version of the title story published by Holt, Rinehart & Winston in New York and Rupert Hart-Davis in London: Arthur Cohen, whose idea it was; Jim Dine, who illustrated it; Robert Cornfield, who helped see it through; members of the Institute for International Education, who administered the Fulbright that gave me a year in Paris, in 1965–66, when this project began; and Christine Tysh, Lawrence Bensky, Kenward Elmslie, Carol Sims, and Elaine Desautel, who read early versions and made many good suggestions.

Gratitude is also due to Serge Fauchereau and Harry Mathews, who helped with difficult spots in the shorter stories, and who set standards of excellence in their own work.

The staffs of the New York Public Library and the Bibliothèque Littéraire Jacques Doucet in Paris were unfailingly helpful, particularly François Chapon.

I would also like to thank Leroy C. Breunig, of the Barnard French

Department, for his encouragement, advice, and congeniality, and Michel Décaudin, whose editions of Apollinaire are models of scholarship. His dazzling and invaluable erudition on the subject of Apollinaire cast light on some very obscure points, rescuing me time and again.

I owe a very great debt of gratitude to Nicole Ball, who not only painstakingly checked the entire translation but also offered excellent and specific rewordings. Her collaboration dramatically improved this translation, which is, in a real sense, hers as well as mine.

This translation was supported in part by a grant from the National Endowment for the Arts, for which I am grateful.

I am also grateful to the editors who accepted some of these stories for publication in their magazines: Trevor Winkfield, Michael Friedman, Gary Lenhart, Greg Masters, Michael Scholnick, and Harry Lewis.

Finally, I wish to express my appreciation to Jack Shoemaker and Tom Christensen at North Point Press, who have done a wonderful job of resuscitating *Le Poète assassiné.*

R.P.

THE POET ASSASSINATED

AND OTHER STORIES

THE POET ASSASSINATED

TO RENÉ DALIZE

1. *Name*

The glory of Croniamantal is today universal. One hundred and twenty-three towns in seven countries on four continents vie for the honor of having seen the birth of this remarkable hero. I shall attempt, further on, to elucidate this important question.

All of these peoples have more or less modified the sonorous name of Croniamantal. The Arabs, the Turks, and other peoples who read from right to left have not failed to pronounce it Latnamainorc, but the Turks, oddly, call him Pata, which means goose or virile organ, as you wish. The Russians surname him Viperdoc, that is, born of a fart; the reason for this nickname will be seen later on. The Scandinavians, or at least the Dalecarlians, readily call him *quoniam*, in Latin, which means *because*, but often indicates the noble parts in the popular tales of the Middle Ages. One notices that the Saxons and the Turks manifest the same spirit in regard to Croniamantal by giving identical surnames (but whose origins are still poorly explained). One supposes that it is a euphemistic allusion to what was found in Croniamantal's death certificate made out by Doctor Ratiboul of Marseille. According to that official document, all of Croniamantal's organs were healthy and the medical expert added, in Latin, as the assistant medical officer Henry did for Napoleon: *partes viriles exiguitatis insignis, sicut pueri.*

After all, there are those countries where the notion of Croniamantalesque virility has completely disappeared. So it is that in Moriania the blacks call him Tsatsa or Dzadza or Rsoussour, feminine names, because they have feminized Croniamantal just as the Byzantines feminized Good Friday by making it Sainte-Parascève.

2. *Procreation*

Two leagues from Spa, on a road lined with bushes and twisted trees, Viersélin Tigoboth, an itinerant musician who was coming from Liège on foot, took the opportunity of lighting his pipe while resting his hot feet. A woman's voice cried out:

"Hey! Mister!"

He raised his head and a wild laugh burst forth:

"Hahaha! Hohoho! Heeheehee! Your eyelids are the color of lentils from Egypt! My name is Macarée. I want a tom."

Viersélin Tigoboth perceived on the side of the road a dark young woman, shaped with pretty globes. How graceful she was in her short biking skirt! Holding her bike with one hand while she gathered tart sloes with the other, she fixed her large, fervent, golden eyes on the Walloon musician.

"Y'arr a boony lassie," said Viersélin Tigoboth, rolling his tongue. "But, nom di Dio, if you eat sloes you'll have the colic tonight, likely."

"I want a tom," repeated Macarée, and undoing her blouse, she showed Viersélin Tigoboth her breasts, similar to the buttocks of angels, with aureoles the soft color of pink clouds at sundown.

"Oh! Oh!" said Viersélin Tigoboth, "they're as beautiful as the pearls of the Amblève, give them to me. I'll go gather you a big bouquet of fern and moon-colored iris."

Viersélin Tigoboth moved forward to seize that miraculous flesh offered him for nothing, like the blessed bread at Mass; but he restrained himself.

"Y'arr a boony froggie di nom di Dio, y'arr boony as the fair at Liège. Y'arr a boonier lass than Donnaye, than Tatenne, than Victoria, whose gallant I was, boonier than the wenches of Mt. Renier who are for sale all the day long. But if ye fly into my arms, my dove, nom di Dio, ye'll fly away a stork."

MACARÉE

"They're the color of the moon
And round as the wheel of Fortune."

VIERSÉLIN TIGOBOTH

"If you're not afraid of catching a louse,
Or two or three, today I'd like to be your spouse."

And Viersélin Tigoboth moved forth, his lips full of kisses:
"I luve ye! It's quiet here! O! Beloved!"

Soon there was nothing there but sighs, birds singing, and horned, reddish-brown rabbits going past, fast little devils, fast as seven-league boots, near Viersélin Tigoboth and Macarée, under love's power, behind the blackthorns.

Then, the bike took Macarée away.

And sad unto death, Viersélin Tigoboth damned the instrument of speed that rolled away and was swallowed behind the terraqueous rotundity, just as the musician began to piss, humming a pasquinade. . . .

3. *Gestation*

Macarée soon realized that she had conceived by Viersélin Tigoboth.

"How unfortunate," she thought at first, "but medicine has made a lot of progress. I'll unload whenever I wish. Ah! That Walloon! He will have labored in vain. Can Macarée bring up the son of a vagabond? No, no, I condemn this embryo to death. I don't even want to preserve it in alcohol, this foetus of bad blood. And you, my belly, if you knew how I love you since I knew your goodness. What? You accept carrying fardels you find along the road? Innocent belly, you are unworthy of my selfish soul.

"What am I saying, O my belly? You are cruel, you separate children from their fathers. No! I don't love you anymore. Now you're just a full sack, O my belly smiling at the navel, O my stretchy, bearded, smooth, bombed, dolorous, round, silky, ennobling belly. Because you do ennoble me, I had forgotten that, O my belly more beautiful than the sun. You would also ennoble the child of the vagrant Walloon—you're worth the thigh of Jupiter. How horrible! A little more and I would have destroyed a child of noble lineage, my child who already is alive inside my beloved belly."

She flung open the door and yelled:

"Madame Dehan! Mademoiselle Baba!"

There was a crashing of doors and locks, and Macarée's landladies came running.

"I'm pregnant," cried Macarée, "I'm pregnant!"

She was sitting on the bed, her legs apart, her skin delicate. Macarée had a small waist and wide hips.

"You poor little thing," said Madame Dehan, who had one eye, a moustache, was hip-shot and lame. "You poor little thing, you don't know what you're in for. After the delivery, women are like June–bug shells, which crackle under the feet of people walking by. After the delivery, women are just a box of maladies (look at me!), eggshells full of spells, incantations, and other voodoos. Ah! Ah! You've certainly done a good job!"

"Nonsense!" said Macarée. "A woman's duty is to have children and I know for a fact that generally it has a very happy effect on their health mental *and* physical."

"Which side are you sick on?" asked Mademoiselle Baba.

"Be quiet, O.K.!?" said Madame Dehan. "Instead, go look for my vial of Spa elixir and bring some little glasses too."

Mademoiselle Baba brought in the elixir. They drank some.

"That's better," said Madame Dehan. "After such an emotional moment I needed a restorative."

She poured herself another little glass of elixir, drank it, and caught the last droplets with her tongue.

"Imagine," she said then, "imagine, Madame Macarée. . . . I swear on what I hold most sacred in this world, as Mademoiselle Baba is my witness, this is the first time such a thing has happened to one of my tenants. And there have been plenty of them all right! Louise Bernier, they called her The Fold because she was so flat; Marcelle Wac (whose insolence was stunning!); Joshuette, who died of heat exhaustion she took in Christiania, the sun taking its revenge on Joshua; Lili de Murkery, a great name, so it seems (not hers naturally), and then rather unpleasant for a chic woman, as she might put it: 'You must pronounce it Mercury,' she used to say with her mouth looking like the asshole of a chicken. And do you know, she ended up like that—they filled her full of mercury like a thermometer. In the morning she used to ask me: 'What's the weather to be like today?' But I always answered: 'You should know better than me. . . .' Never, absolutely never were they pregnant here at my place."

"Well, O.K., but let's get back to the matter at hand," said Macarée. "I've never been either. Give me some advice, but make it short."

At that moment she got up.

"Oh!" cried Madame Dehan, "what a marvelous behind you have! How dazzling! What whiteness! What plumpness! Mademoiselle Baba, Madame Macarée is going to put on her dressing gown. Serve the coffee and bring in the huckleberry tart too."

Macarée put on a top and then slipped into a dressing gown whose belt was a plaid scarf.

Mademoiselle Baba returned; on a large tray she carried the cups, the coffee pot, the milk pitcher, the honey pot, slices of buttered bread, and the huckleberry tart.

"You want some good advice?" said Madame Dehan while using the back of her hand to wipe off the café au lait that was running down her chin. "Have the child baptized."

"I will," said Macarée.

"I even think," said Mademoiselle Baba, "that it would be a good idea to sprinkle it the day it's born."

"That's right," mumbled Madame Dehan, her mouth full, "you never know what might happen. Then you will nurse it yourself, and if I were you, if I had your money, I'd try to go to Rome to be blessed by the Pope before having the baby. It will never know a father's caresses, or punishment, your child; it will never pronounce the sweet name of papa. At least let the Pope's benediction follow it all its life."

And Madame Dehan began to sob like a stew boiling over. Macarée poured forth tears as abundant as those of a spouting whale. But what can one say of Mademoiselle Baba? Her lips blue with huckleberries, she wept harder and harder so that the sobs spread from her throat down to her maidenhead, which nearly choked itself.

4. *Nobility*

After having won a lot of money at baccarat, and already rich thanks to Love, Macarée, whose bulge still didn't show, went to Paris, where the first thing she did was go shopping at the stylish designers'.

O she was chic! O she was chic!

▪

One evening when she went to the Théâtre-Français they were doing a play with a message. In the first act, a young lady rendered sterile by surgery was caring for the largeness of her dropsical and extremely jealous husband. The doctor went away saying:

"A great miracle and a great devotion are all that can save him."

In the second act the young lady told the doctor:

"I want to sacrifice myself for my husband. I want to become dropsical in his place."

"Let us love, madame. If you are not unsuitable for maternity, your wish will be fulfilled. And what a sweet glory it will be for me!"

"Alas!" murmured the young lady, "I no longer have any ovaries."

"Love," cried the doctor then, "love, madame, is capable of working many miracles."

In the third act, the husband, thin as an I and the lady, eight months pregnant, congratulated each other on the exchange they had made. The doctor presented to the Academy his findings on the fertilization of women rendered sterile by surgery.

▪

Near the end of the third act someone in the audience shouted: "Fire!" The frightened spectators ran screaming toward the exits. Macarée latched onto the arm of the first man she met. He was well dressed and handsome, and since Macarée was charming he seemed flattered that she had chosen him as her protector. They struck up an acquaintance at a cafe and from there went to dine in Montmartre. But it so happened that François des Ygrées had thoughtlessly forgotten his wallet. Macarée willingly paid the bill. And François des Ygrées extended his gallantry so far as to express his wish that Macarée, whom the fire incident had unnerved, should not sleep alone.

▪

François Baron des Ygrées (false barony, besides) described himself as the last scion of a noble house of Provence and professed heraldry from the seventh floor of a building in the rue Charles V.

"But," he said, "revolutions and demagogues have done so much that heraldry is now studied only by common archeologists, while the nobles are no longer indoctrinated in that art."

The Baron des Ygrées, whose coat of arms was *azure with three silver palls set in the pale*, was able to inspire enough sympathy in Macarée that, out of gratitude for the night at the Théâtre-Français, she wanted to take heraldry lessons.

Macarée showed herself, it's true, little inclined to retain the terms of heraldry, and one can say that her only serious interest was in the arms of the Pignatelli family, who have furnished popes to the Church and whose coat of arms is furnished with pots.

Nevertheless, these lessons were a waste of time for neither Macarée nor for François des Ygrées, since they ended by getting married. As her dowry Macarée brought her money, her beauty, and her pregnancy. François des Ygrées offered Macarée a great name and his noble bearing.

Neither of them found anything to complain about in the bargain and they were happy.

"Macarée, my dear wife," said François des Ygrées a few days after their marriage, "why have you ordered so much clothing? It seems to me that not one day goes by but the dressmakers are bringing something new. It's true they do honour to your good taste and to their abilities."

Macarée hesitated a moment, then replied:

"It's for our wedding trip, François!"

"Our wedding trip, I had been considering it. But where do you count on going?"

"To Rome," said Macarée.

"To Rome, like the Easter beggars?"

"I want to see the Pope," said Macarée.

"Very nice, but for what purpose?"

"So that he may bless the child who kicks in my womb," said Macarée.

"Zounds! 'Swounds!"

"It will be your son," said Macarée.

"You're right, Macarée. We'll go to Rome, like the Easter beggars. You'll order a new black velvet gown; and let's make sure that the dressmaker has our allusive arms embroidered at the bottom of the skirt: *azure with three silver palls set in the pale.*"

5. *Papacy*

"Per carità, my lady *baroness* (I'd willingly call you miss!). Ah! Ah! Ah! but your husband the *baron*, he would protest, ah! ah! ah! It's true, you have a little belly which is beginning to grow overbearing. They work hard in France, I see. Ah, if that beautiful country wished to become religious again, immediately the population, decimated by anticlericalism (yes, *baroness*, it's a proven fact), the population would increase considerably. Ah! Holy Jesus! How well she listens, the arrogantine. Ah! ah! ah! So you want to see the Pope. Ah! ah! The benediction of a simple cardinal like myself is not enough. Ah! ah! Not a word, I understand quite well. Ah! ah! I'll try to obtain an audience. Oh! Don't thank me, leave my hand alone please. How well she kisses, the arrogantine, well! yes! Come here again, I want you to take away a little souvenir of me.

"There! a chain with the medallion of the holy house of Loretto. May I ass you if . . . I mean . . . Ah! this French, we can't pronounce it . . . *ask* you if you will accept this? . . . There, now that you have the medallion you must promise me you'll always keep it. Good, good, good! Come here so I can kiss you on the forehead. There! Come, come, is the arrogantine afraid of me? There! What's so funny . . . Nothing! Well! Some advice! When you go to the Vatican, I suggest that you don't wear so much stink, I mean scent. Good-bye, arrogantine. Come see me again. My compliments to the *baron*."

▪

And so, thanks to Cardinal Ricottino, who had been the nuncio at Paris, Macarée obtained a papal audience.

She went to the Vatican dressed in her beautiful emblazoned gown. The Baron des Ygrées, in a frock coat, accompanied her. He greatly admired the uniforms of the High Guard, and the Swiss mercenaries, inclined to drinking bouts and mutiny, seemed handsome devils to him. He took the opportunity to whisper to his wife about one of his ancestors who had been a cardinal under Louis XIII. . . .

▪

The couple returned to the hotel very moved, steeped in the papal benediction. They undressed chastely, and in bed they talked at length about the Pontiff, the white head of the Church, that snow the Catholics believe eternal, a greenhouse lily.

"My wife," concluded François des Ygrées, "I adore you and at the same time I have great esteem for you, and I shall love with all my heart the child who has been blessed by the Pope. May the blessed child come, but I want it to be born in France."

"François," said Macarée, "I've never been to Monte Carlo, let's go there! I won't lose my marbles. We're not millionaires. I'm certain I'll be successful in Monte Carlo."

"Zounds! 'Swounds! The deuce!" swore François, "Macarée, you make me see red."

"Ouch!" cried Macarée, "you kicked me, you pim. . . ."

"I'm glad to see, Macarée," said François des Ygrées wittily, quickly regaining his composure, "that you have not forgotten that I am your husband."

"Come my little zozo, we leave for Monaco."

"Yes, but you'll give birth in France, because Monaco is an independent state."

"O.K.," said Macarée.

The next day the Baron des Ygrées and the Baroness, all swollen with mosquito bites, went to the station and bought their tickets for Monaco. In the compartment they made some charming plans.

6. *Gambrinus*

The Baron and Baroness des Ygrées, when buying tickets for Monaco, thought they would arrive at that station which is the fifth when one goes from Italy to France and the second in the little principality of Monaco.

The name Monaco is properly the Italian name of that principality, although it's used by the French today, the French designations Mourgues and Monèghe having fallen into desuetude.

Now, in Italian, Monaco not only means the principality of that name, but also the capital of Bavaria which the French call Munich. The employee had given the Baron tickets for Monaco-Munich instead of Monaco-principality. When the Baron and the Baroness realized the error, they were already at the Swiss frontier, and after recovering from their astonishment, decided to go on to Munich to see firsthand everything that the anti-artistic, modern German spirit has been able to conceive in the way of ugliness in architecture, statuary, painting, and decorative arts. . . .

▪

A cold March caused the couple to shiver in that cardboard Athens. . . .

"Beer," the Baron des Ygrées had said, "is excellent for pregnant women."

He took his wife to the Royal Pschorr Brewery, to the Augustinerbrau, to the Munchnerkindl, and to other breweries.

They climbed the Nockerberg where there's a large garden. The most famous March beer, the *Salvator*, is drunk there, as long as it lasts, which isn't long, because the people of Munich are drunkards.

▪

When the Baron entered the garden with his wife, they found it overrun with a mob of already soused drinkers, who were singing at the top of their voices and dancing the brawl and breaking their empty mugs.

Vendors were selling roast poultry, grilled herring, pretzels, rolls, pork, sweets, souvenir trinkets, and postal cards. Also, Hannes Irlbeck, the King of Drinkers, was there. Since Perkes, the dwarf-drunkard of the great barrel of Heidelberg, the earth had not seen such a fish. Through the March beer, then through the bock beer in May, Hannes Irlbeck drank his forty quarts of beer. Ordinarily he drank only twenty-five.

Just as the graceful des Ygrées couple walked by him, Hannes sat his colossal buttocks on a bench, which, already supporting at least twenty enormous men and women, cracked immediately. The drinkers fell legs in the air. Noticeable were several naked thighs, since women's stockings in Munich go no higher than the knee. Laughter erupted everywhere. Hannes Irlbeck, who had also toppled over, but without letting go of his mug, poured its contents out on the belly of a girl who had rolled over near him, and the beer foaming under her resembled what she did as soon as she was standing, while gulping down a quart nonstop in order to recover her wits.

But the garden's manager yelled:

"Donnerkeil! Stupid pigs . . . a broken bench."

And he rushed forward with his towel under his arm while calling the waiters:

"Franz! Jacob! Ludwig! Martin!" while the customers called the manager:

"Ober! Ober!"

Still, the Oberkellner and the waiters did not return. The drinkers pressed in at the counters where you fill your own mug, but the barrels would give forth no more; no longer did you hear from minute to minute the sonorous bangs which announced the tapping of a new cask. The singing had stopped, the angry drinkers yelled insults at the bartenders and against the March beer itself. Others were taking advantage of the intermission by vomiting wildly, their eyes bulging out of their heads; their neighbors would encourage them with an imperturbable seriousness. Hannes Irlbeck, who had gotten back on his feet, but not without great effort, sniffed and murmured:

"There's no more beer in Munich!"

And he repeated in the accent of his hometown:

"Minchen! Minchen! Minchen!"

And having raised his eyes to the sky, he flung himself toward a poultry stand, where he ordered a roasted goose and began to fantasize.

"No more beer in Munich . . . if only there were some white radishes!"

And he repeated at length the term they use in Munich:

"Raadi, raadi, raadi. . . ."

Suddenly he stopped. The mob of thirsty drinkers gave out a cry of satisfaction. The four waiters had just appeared in the doorway of the bar. It was with great dignity they were carrying a sort of canopy under which the Oberkellner walked as proud and straight as a dethroned African king. They were preceding new barrels of beer, which were tapped in time with the bell, while laughing, shouting, and singing erupted from that seething hill, hard and agitated as Adam de Gambrinus' Adam's apple itself, when, ridiculously dressed as a monk, a white radish in one hand, he uses the other to turn up the jug which delights his gullet.

And the child to come was jostled about by Macarée's laughing at the stupendous guzzling; and she completely quenched her own thirst as did her husband.

Now, the mother's happiness had a happy influence on the character of her descendant, who even before his birth acquired a lot of good sense from it, and true good sense, I mean, that of the great poets.

7. *Delivery*

The Baron François des Ygrées left Munich the moment the Baroness Macarée knew that the hour of delivery was approaching. Mister des Ygrées did not want a child born in Bavaria; he asserted that that country predisposes one to syphilis.

They arrived with the spring in the little port of Machique, which the Baron baptized for eternity with a lyrical pun whose effect was most beautiful:

Machique with golden skies.

It is there the delivery took place.

▪

"Ah! Ah! Ouch! Ouch! Ouch! Ay! Ay! Agghh!"

The three midwives took to chatting pleasantly:

FIRST MIDWIFE

"I am thinking of the war.

O my friends, the stars, the beautiful stars, have you counted them?

O my friends, do you remember even the titles of all the books you've read and the names of the authors?

O my friends, have you thought of the poor men who built the broad highways?

The shepherds of the Golden Age let their flocks out to pasture without fearing the *abigeat*, they feared only the wild beasts.

O my friends, what do you think of all these cannons?"

SECOND MIDWIFE

"What do I think of all these cannons? They are vigorous phalli.

O my beautiful nights! I'm happy with a sinister crow that enchanted me last night, it's a good omen. My hair's perfumed with able-musk.

O the beautiful and unbending phalli which these cannons are! If women had had to do military service, they would have joined the artillery. The sight of cannons must be strange during a battle.

Lights are born far out on the sea.

Reply, O Zelotide, reply with your sweet voice."

THIRD MIDWIFE

"I love his eyes in the night and he knows my hair and its smell. In the streets of Marseille an officer followed me a long time. He was well dressed and rosy-cheeked, he had gold on his clothes, and his mouth tempted me, but I fled his kisses and took refuge in thē or thĕ boarding house where I lived."

FIRST MIDWIFE

"O Zelotide, spare the sad men as you spared this dandy. Zelotide, what do you think of the cannons?"

SECOND MIDWIFE

"Alas! Alas! I should like to be loved."

THIRD MIDWIFE

"They are the instruments of the ignoble love of the people. O Sodom! Sodom! O sterile love!"

FIRST MIDWIFE

"But we are women, and what are you saying about Sodom?"

THIRD MIDWIFE

"The fire from the sky devoured it."

THE ONE IN LABOR

"When you've finished your putting us on, if it doesn't put you off, don't forget to get busy with the Baroness des Ygrées."

■

The Baron was sleeping on a few travel blankets in a corner of the room. He farted, which made his better half laugh till she cried. Macarée was weeping, screaming, laughing, and a few moments later giving the world a healthy, masculine child. Then, exhausted by all these efforts, she gave up the ghost, giving a howl similar to that ululation Adam's eternal first wife gives as she crosses the Red Sea.

In reporting what precedes, I think I have elucidated the important question of the birthplace of Croniamantal. Let the hundred twenty-three towns* in seven countries on four continents vie for the honor of having given birth to him.

We now know, and the civil registers are there for once, that he was born of the paternal fart, in *Machique with golden skies*, August 25, 1889, but wasn't registered at the city hall until the next morning.

It was the year of the Universal Exposition, and the Eiffel Tower, which had just been born, saluted the heroic birth of Croniamantal with a handsome erection.

The Baron des Ygrées farted again, which awakened him, near the macabre bed where in mock array was Macarée laid out in an imposing way. The child was crying, the midwives were clucking, the father sobbing, crying:

"Ah! Machique with golden skies, I've killed my chickie with golden eyes!"

Then he baptized the newly born, giving him a name that he immediately invented and which belongs to no saint in paradise: CRONIAMANTAL. He left the next day, after having arranged for his wife's funeral, written the letters necessary for the inheritance, and declared the child under the names Gaétan-François-Etienne-Jack-Amélie-Alonso Desygrées. With this infant whose putative father he was, he took the train for the Principality of Monaco.

8. *Mammon*

Now a widower, François des Ygrées moved in near the principality. In the district of Roquebrune he took room and board with a family,

*Among these towns, we cite Naples, Adrianople, Constantinople, Neauphle-le-Château, Grenoble, Pultava, Pouilly-en-Auxois, Pouilly-les-Fleurs, Nauplia, Seoul, Melbourne, Oran, Nazareth, Ermenonville, Nogent-sur-Marne, etc.

part of which was a pretty brunette named Mia. There he himself bottle-fed the heir to his name.

He often went for a stroll at dawn beside the sea. The road was bordered with guavas which, each time he saw them, he involuntarily compared to packages of dried cod. Sometimes, due to contrary winds, he turned around to light an Egyptian cigarette whose smoke rose in spirals similar to the bluish mountains that blurred in the distance in Italy.

▪

The family he had moved in with consisted of the father, the mother, and Mia. Mr. Cecchi, a Corsican, was a croupier at the Casino. He had formerly been a croupier at Baden-Baden and there had married a German woman. From that union was born Mia, whose dark skin and hair especially bore witness to her Corsican blood. She was always dressed in loud colors. Her gait was rolling, her chest thrust out; she had less bosom than bottom, and a mild case of strabism gave her dark eyes a slightly distraught look, which made her only more desirable.

Her speech was slack and soft and she gargled her r's, but it was nonetheless agreeable. This is the Monacan accent, whose syntax Mia also used. After he saw the young girl picking roses a few times, François des Ygrées became interested in her; and he was amused by that syntax whose rules it pleased him to seek. First he noticed the Italianisms and above all the one that consists in conjugating the verb "to be" with itself as an auxiliary, instead of using the verb "to have." Thus, Mia would say, "I was been" instead of "I have been." He noted that strange rule which consists in repeating the verb of the main clause after the clause: "I was been in Moulins while you were going to Menton, I was been," or: "This year I want to go to Nice for the calabash fair, I want."

▪

Once, before sunrise, François des Ygrées went down into the garden. There he abandoned himself to a sweet daydream, during which he caught a cold. Suddenly he began sneezing twenty times in a row, achee, achoo, achee.

These sneezes loosened him up. He saw the sky turning white and dawn appearing first on the sea's horizon. Then dawn began flaming in the sky in the direction of Italy. The still gloomy sea extended in the other direction, and on the horizon, like a little cloud flush with the sea, the summits of Corsica, which disappear after sunup, curved down. The Baron des Ygrées shivered, then he yawned stretching. Then he looked back at the sea in the east where a royal flotilla seemed to blaze in sight of a sea town with white houses, Bordighere, which furnishes the palms for the celebrations at the Vatican. He turned toward the motionless guardian of the garden: this great cypress with a garland of rose bushes climbing to the top. François des Ygrées inhaled the sumptuous roses whose fragrance was unparalleled and whose still-closed petals were fleshy.

At that moment Mia called him for breakfast.

With her braid down her back, she had just picked some figs and was letting some milky drops fall from them into a bowl of milk. She smiled at François des Ygrées, saying, "Would you like a taste of curdled milk?" He said no, because he didn't like it.

"Did you have a nice rest?" she asked.

"No, there are too many mosquitoes."

"You know, when they bite you, you just have to rub it with a lemon and to not be stung you put some vaseline on your face before you go to bed. They never bite me."

"That would be too bad. Because you are very pretty and you must have been told so, often."

"There are some who say so and others who think so without saying it, there are. For those who say so, it leaves me neither hot nor cold, for the others it's just too bad for them, it is . . ."

And François des Ygrées immediately thought up a fable for the timid ones:

The Fable of the Oyster and the Herring

A beautiful and wise oyster lived on a rock. She did not dream of love, but on beautiful days gaped beatifically at the sun. A herring saw her and it was love at first sight. He fell head over heels in love with her, without daring to confess it to her.

One summer day, happy and settled, the oyster was gaping. Cowering behind a rock, the herring was contemplating her, but all at once the desire to give his beloved a kiss became so strong that he could not resist it.

And so he threw himself between the open shells of the oyster and, surprised, she suddenly clamped them shut, decapitating the poor herring, whose headless body began to float this way and that, on the ocean.

"So much the worse for the herring," said Mia, laughing. "He was too stupid. Now I like it when they say I'm pretty, but not for fun, but so we can get him engaged. . . ."

And François des Ygrées made a mental note of this curious particularity of syntax which conjugates the plural of the pronominal verbs with the sole aid, for each person, of the reflexive pronoun of the third person: we get him engaged, you get him engaged. . . . And he thought again:

"She doesn't love me. Macarée dead. Mia indifferent. It's plain to see I'm unlucky in love."

▪

One day he happened to be in the little valley of Gaumates, on a hillock planted with little scrubby pines. The coast edged with the blue white of the waves stretched out into the distance in front of him. The Casino emerged from the forest of rare trees in its gardens. François des Ygrées looked at it. The palace resembled a crouching man raising his arms to the sky. François des Ygrées heard an invisible Mammon near him:

"Look at that palace, François, it is made in the image of man. It is social like him. It likes those who visit it and above all those unlucky in love. Go there and you will win, because people can't lose at gambling when they're unlucky in love, as you are."

As it was six o'clock, the angelus rang in the different churches of the vicinity. The voice of the bells prevailed against the voice of the invisible Mammon who was now silent, while François des Ygrées searched for him.

▪

The next day François des Ygrées took the road to the temple of Mammon. It was Palm Sunday. The streets were crammed with children, girls, and women carrying palms and olive boughs. The palms were either plain or woven according to a special art. At each corner, palm weavers were working seated against a wall. Under their expert fingers the fibers of the palms bent and coiled strangely and gracefully. Children were already playing with hard-boiled eggs. In a square a bunch of kids was giving a redheaded kid a thrashing because they had caught him using a marble egg. That's how he broke the eggs and won them. Little tiny girls were going to Mass, well-dressed and bearing, like candles, woven palms on which their mothers had hung delicacies.

François des Ygrées thought:

"The sight of palms brings good luck and today is Palm Sunday, I'm going to break the bank."

▪

In the gaming hall he first watched the disparate crowd press around the tables. . . .

François des Ygrées approached a table and played it. He lost. The invisible Mammon had returned and would say harshly each time the chips were raked in:

"You lost!"

And François no longer saw the crowd; his head was spinning; he bet coins, wads of bills, played street, straight, split, on color. He played a long time, losing all he could.

He finally turned around and saw the shining hall where the players thronged as before. Spying a young man whose sullen face indicated that he hadn't had much luck, François smiled at him and asked him if he'd lost.

The young man said furiously:

"You too? A Russian won over two hundred thousand francs right next to me. Oh! If I still had a hundred francs I'd go get myself together at trente et quarante. Well then no, in fact, I have lousy luck, really rotten luck, I'm screwed. Imagine. . . ."

And taking François by the arm he pulled him over to a divan on which they sat down.

"Imagine," he continued, "I've lost everything. I'm almost a thief. The money I lost didn't belong to me. I'm not rich. I have a good job in business. My boss sent me to pick up some checks in Marseille. I cashed them. I took the train to come try my luck. I lost. So now I'll be arrested. They'll say I'm dishonest, but I haven't profited from that money. I lost it all. Had I won? No one would have said a thing. Oh! What lousy luck! There's nothing for me to do but kill myself."

And suddenly, standing up, the young man brought a revolver to his mouth and fired. The body was taken out. A few players turned slightly but no one moved aside and most of them didn't even notice the incident, which made a profound impression on the mind of Baron des Ygrées. He had lost everything Macarée had left him and which was destined for his child. Leaving, François felt the universe closing around him like a cell, then like a coffin. He got back to the villa where he lived. At the door he stopped in front of Mia, who was chatting with a traveler with a suitcase in his hand.

"I'm Dutch," the man was saying, "but I live in Provence and I'd like to rent a room for a few days; I've come here to make some mathematical observations."

At this moment the Baron des Ygrées blew a kiss to Mia with his left hand and with a revolver in his right he blew out his brains and crashed into the dust.

"We have only one room," said Mia, "but it's free now."

And she quickly closed the Baron's eyes, started squawking like a magpie, and the whole neighborhood came running. They went for the police, who took the body away, and the whole thing was never mentioned again.

▪

As for the young child, whom his father, in a burst of lyricism peculiar to him had named once and for all Croniamantal, he was given a home by the Dutch traveler, who soon took him away to rear him as his own son.

The day they left, Mia sold her virginity to a millionaire crack skeet shooter, which was the thirty-fifth time she had indulged in that little commercial operation.

9. *Pedagogy*

The Dutchman, who was named Janssen, took Croniamantal to the outskirts of Aix, to a house the people of the area called the Castle.

There was nothing lordly about the Castle except its name; it was just a vast residence with a dairy and a stable.

Mr. Janssen had a comfortable income and lived alone in this house he had bought so he could live to the side of things; his engagement, abruptly broken, had made him a bit of a hypochondriac. He now devoted his resources to the education of the son of Macarée and Viersélin Tigoboth: Croniamantal, the inheritor of the old name of des Ygrées.

▪

The Dutchman Janssen had traveled widely. He spoke all the languages of Europe—Arabic, Turkish, not to mention Hebrew and the other dead languages. His speech was as clear as his blue eyes. He had quickly made friends with a few humanists in Aix, whom he sometimes visited, and he corresponded with many foreign scholars.

When Croniamantal turned six, Mr. Janssen often took him out in the country in the morning. Croniamantal loved these lessons along the paths of the bosky hills. Mr. Janssen would stop sometimes, and pointing to the birds fluttering near one another, or the butterflies chasing each other and fluttering together on an eglantine, he would say that love guides all nature. They would also go out in the evening under the moonlight where the master would explain to his student the secret destinies of the stars, their regular courses, and their effects on men.

Croniamantal never forgot one moonlit evening in May when his master had led him to a field at the edge of a forest. The grass was streaming with a milky light. The lightning bugs pulsed around them, their wandering and phosphorescent glimmers giving the place an eerie look. The master drew his disciple's attention to the mildness of that May night:

"Learn," he said to the boy, "learn about all nature and love it. May it be your veritable wetnurse, whose illustrious breasts are the moon and the hill."

At that time Croniamantal was thirteen and his mind was quite alert. He listened attentively to Mr. Janssen's words.

"I've always lived in it, but all in all lived badly, because one should not live without human love, without a companion. Do not forget that everything is proof of love in nature. I myself, alas! I am damned for not having followed that law, before which there exists only its necessity, which is destiny."

"How is it," said Croniamantal, "that you, my master, who know so much science, you have not honored this law even though bumpkins understand it and even the animals, vegetables, and inert matter?"

"Lucky child who at thirteen can ask such a question!" said Mr. Janssen. "I have always known this law, against which no being can rebel. But a few unfortunate men must not know love. That is particularly the case with poets and scholars. Souls are like little vagabonds; I am aware of the previous lives of my soul. It has never animated anything but the sterile bodies of scholars. There should be nothing surprising about that. Entire races respect the animals and proclaim metempsychosis, an honorable belief, evident, but exaggerated, since it does not take into account lost forms and the inevitable dispersal. Their respect should have been extended to vegetables and even to minerals. The dust of the road, what is it but the ashes of the dead? It is true that the Ancients did not ascribe life to inert things. Rabbis have thought that the same soul inhabited the bodies of Adam, Moses, and David. In fact, the name Adam is composed in Hebrew of Aleph, Daleth, and Mem, the first letters of the three names. Yours lived as did mine in other human bodies, in other animals, or was dispersed and will continue after your death since all must be used again. Because perhaps there is nothing new and creation has perhaps ceased. . . . I add that I have not wanted love, but I swear, I would not begin another life like this one. I have mortified my flesh and practiced hard penances. I would like you to have a happy life."

Croniamantal's master had him devote the major part of his time to the sciences; he kept him up to date on the new inventions. He also taught him Latin and Greek. Often, they read Virgil's eclogues or translated Theocritus in a grove of olive trees similar to those of antiquity. Croniamantal had learned a very pure French, but the master taught in Latin; he acquainted him with Italian too and soon gave him the rimes of Petrarch, who became one of his favorite poets. Mr. Janssen also taught Croniamantal English and familiarized him with Shakespeare. Above all, he gave him a taste for the old French authors. Among the French poets, he particularly admired Villon, Ronsard and his Pléiade, Racine, and La Fontaine. He also had him read translations of Cervantes and Goethe. On his advice Croniamantal read novels of chivalry, some of which could have been part of Don Quixote's library. They developed in Croniamantal an insurmountable taste for adventure and perilous love; he busied himself with fencing and horsemanship; at the age of fifteen he declared to every visitor that he had decided to become a famous knight who knows no master, and already he was dreaming of a mistress.

Croniamantal was, at that time, a handsome adolescent, slender and straight. When he brushed against the girls at the village festivals, they stifled their giggles and blushed and lowered their eyes under his gaze. His mind, accustomed to poetic forms, conceived of love as a conquest. Reminiscences of Boccaccio, his bold nature, his education, all predisposed him to daring.

One May day he had gone for a long ride. It was morning and nature was still fresh. The dew hung from the flowers on the bushes and on each side of the road stretched fields of olive trees whose gray leaves moved quietly in the sea breeze and were agreeably wedded with the celestial blue. He came to a spot where work was being done on the road. The workers, handsome boys in beautifully colored caps, were working lazily, singing and stopping to take an occasional swig from their gourds. Croniamantal thought that these fellows had misty-eyed girlfriends, for around there the boys and girls say "my pet." Perhaps he did not understand their dialect so well, and in fact the girls and the boys in that beautiful region do pet a lot. Croniamantal felt infinitely sad and his whole being, exalted by springtime and the ride he'd taken, cried out for love.

At a bend in the road, an apparition increased his pain. He came to a little bridge thrown over a river that cut the road. It was a solitary place and, through the bushes and the poplar trunks, he saw two beautiful girls bathing, completely naked. One, in the water, was holding onto a branch. He admired her dark arms and plump charms the water hardly veiled. The other, standing on the bank, was drying herself after her bath, her ravishing contours visible, and her graces so enflamed Croniamantal he decided to join these girls and their frolics. Unfortunately he noticed, among the branches of a nearby tree, two striplings watching their prey. Holding their breaths, attentive to the bathers' slightest gestures, they were unaware of the cavalier who, laughing with all his might, threw his horse into a gallop and crossed the little bridge screaming.

▪

The sun had risen, and, near the zenith, shot down its unbearable rays. A burning thirst was added to Croniamantal's anxiety over love. The sight of a farm on the side of the road caused in him an unspeakable joy. He soon came to a little farmhouse, behind which there was a small orchard made delicious by its trees in bloom. It was a little pink and white wood of cherry and peach trees. On the hedge, linen was drying and he had the pleasure of seeing a ravishing peasant girl about sixteen years old, washing some clothes in a tub, in the shadow of a young fig tree which, growing in the next yard, bent over the orchard. Not having noticed his arrival, she continued her domestic functions, which he found noble, because, filled with memories of old, he compared her to Nausicaa. Dismounting, he went over to the hedge and, entranced, stared at the pretty girl. He was seeing her from behind. Her tucked-up petticoats uncovered a finely turned calf in a very white stocking. Her body was jiggling in an agreeably provocative way with the scrubbing. Her sleeves were pulled up and he noticed beautiful dark and dimpled arms, which enchanted him.

▪

I have always particularly loved beautiful arms. There are those people who attach great importance to the perfection of the foot. I admit that I am moved by it too, but the arm is in my opinion what should be most perfect in a woman. It is always moving; it is always in sight. One could say that it is the organ of graces, and, by its adroit motions, it is the veritable arm of Love when, bent, this delicate arm imitates a bow, and when extended, describes an arrow.

▪

This was also Croniamantal's opinion. He was thinking about it when suddenly his horse, which he was holding by the reins, aware of the usual hour for its feed, began neighing for it. The young girl immediately turned around and seemed surprised to see a stranger looking at her over the hedge. Her blushing made her even more charming. Her dark skin bespoke the Saracen blood that ran in her veins. Croniamantal asked her for something to eat and drink. With much good grace, this lovely girl had him enter the dairy where she served him a rustic meal. Milk, eggs, butter, and black bread soon satisfied his hunger and thirst. In the meantime, he questioned his young hostess, in the hope of finding an occasion to utter gallantries to her. Thus, he learned that her name was Mariette and that her parents had gone to the next town to sell vegetables; her brother was working on the road. This family lived happily off the products of the orchard and the barn.

Just then the parents, handsome peasants, arrived and there was Croniamantal, already in love with Mariette, completely disappointed. He took advantage of their return to ask the mother how much he owed. Then he left, after giving Mariette a long, meaningful look, one she did not return; but he did have the pleasure of seeing her blush as she turned away.

He remounted and took the road back toward his house. Being sad with love for the first time, he found an extreme melancholy in the countryside he had crossed earlier. The sun had descended to the horizon. The gray leaves of the olive trees seemed as sad as he. Shadows stretched out like a wave. The river where he'd seen the bathers was deserted. The sound of the little waves was unbearable, like a mocking. He threw his horse into a gallop. Then it was twilight; lights went on in the distance. Then, with night, he slowed his horse and abandoned himself to a disordered dream. The downward sloping road was bordered with cypresses, and so it was, darkened by night and by love, Croniamantal followed the melancholy road.

▪

During the next few days his master easily noticed that he was no longer paying the slightest attention to the studies to which he had previously applied himself. Mr. Janssen guessed that this distaste was the result of love.

His respect was tinged with scorn because Mariette was merely a simple peasant.

The end of September had come, and, having taken Croniamantal out the next day under the olive trees laden with fruit, Mr. Janssen reprimanded his disciple's passion. Croniamantal, red in the face, listened to these reproaches. The first autumn winds were moaning and Croniamantal, very sad and very ashamed, forever lost the desire to see his pretty Mariette again, to keep only the memory of her.

▪

It was thus that Croniamantal reached his adulthood.

He was discharged from the military when it was discovered that he had a heart condition. Soon after, his master died suddenly, leaving in his will what little he possessed to Croniamantal. And after selling the house called the Castle, Croniamantal went to Paris so he could peacefully indulge his taste for literature, because for some time now, and secretly, he was writing poems, which he kept in an old cigar box.

10. *Poetry*

In the first days of the year 1911, a badly dressed young man was running up the rue Houdon. His extremely mobile face seemed by turns joyful and disturbed. His eyes devoured everything they saw and when his eyelids came together rapidly like jaws, they engulfed the universe which was endlessly renovated by him as he ran along imagining the smallest details of the enormous worlds he was feasting his eyes on. The clamor and thunder of Paris boomed out in the distance and around the young man, who stopped, completely winded, like a burglar who's been chased too long and is at last ready to give himself up. These noises meant that the enemies were on the verge of tracking him down like a thief. His mouth and eyes expressed the double—walking slowly now, he took refuge in his memory, and he went on ahead, while all the forces of his destiny and his consciousness dismissed time so that the truth of what is, what was, and what will be might appear.

The young man went into a one-story house. On the open door a sign read:

ATELIER ENTRANCE

He followed a corridor where it was so dark and cold he felt as if he were dying, and with all his will, clenching his teeth and fists, he smashed eternity to smithereens. Then suddenly he again had the notion of time, whose seconds hammered out by a clock he heard were falling like bits of glass, and life picked him up again as time began to pass once more. But just as he was ready to knock on a door, his heart beat harder for fear of finding no one in.

He knocked on the door and yelled:

"It's me, Croniamantal."

And behind the door the heavy steps of a tired man, or one carrying a very heavy load, approached slowly, and when the door opened there was in the sudden light the creation of two beings and their immediate marriage.

In the atelier, which looked like a stable, a huge flock lay scattered about; they were sleeping paintings and the shepherd watching over them smiled to his friend.

On a shelf some stacks of yellow books simulated pats of butter. And closing the rickety door again, the wind led in unknown beings who complained with little tiny cries in the name of grief. All the wolves of distress howled behind the door, ready to devour the flock, the shepherd, and his friend, to prepare on this same spot the foundation of the new Town. But in the atelier there were joys of all colors. A big window took up the northern side and all you could see was sky-blue, like a woman singing. Croniamantal took off his overcoat which fell to the floor like the corpse of a drowned man, and sitting down on a divan, he silently took a good long look at the new canvas sitting on the easel. Dressed in overalls and barefoot, the painter was also looking at the picture where two women were remembered in the icy fog.

There was also a fatal thing in the atelier: this big piece of broken mirror, held to the wall by hook-nails. It was an unfathomable vertical dead sea, in the depths of which a false life animated that which does not exist. Thus, facing Art, there is its appearance, which men believe in and which abases them, whereas Art had elevated them. Still seated, Croniamantal leaned forward, and, forearms on his knees, he looked away from the painting onto a sign thrown on the floor and on which was brushed the following notice:

I'M AT THE BISTRO
The Bird of Benin.

He read and reread that sentence while the Bird of Benin looked at his painting, moving his head, stepping back, coming up close. Then he turned to Croniamantal and said:

"I saw your woman last night."

"Who is it?" asked Croniamantal.

"I don't know, I saw her but I don't know her, she's a real young girl, like you like them. She has the somber, childlike face of those who are destined to cause suffering. I'm telling you, I saw your woman. She is ugliness and beauty; she is like everything we love today. And she must have the taste of bay leaf."

But Croniamantal, who was not listening, interrupted him: "Yesterday I wrote my last poem in regular verse:

Lute
Shoot!

and my last poem in irregular verse.

(Please note that the word *girl* in the second strophe is to be taken in its bad sense.)"

PROSPECTUS FOR A NEW MEDICATION

Why did Hjalmar come back
The fine silver tankards were still empty
The evening stars
Became the morning stars
And vice versa
The witch of the forest of Hruloe
Was fixing dinner
She was a horse-eater
But he was not
Mai Mai ramaho nia nia

Then the morning stars
Became the evening stars again
And vice versa
He cried out—In the name of Maroe
And of his preferred lammergeier
Girl of Arnammoer
Prepare the drink of heroes
—Perfectly noble warrior
Mai Mai ramaho nia nia

She took the sun
And plunged it into the sea
As housewives

Drench a ham in pickling brine
But oh! the voracious pickerel
Have devoured the drowned sun
And have made wigs
From its beams
Mai Mai ramaho nia nia

She took the moon and bandaged it
As is done with the illustrious dead
And little children
And then in the light of only the stars
The eternal ones
She boiled down some salt water
And euphorbia and Norwegian tar
And the snot of Aelves
For our hero to drink
Mai Mai ramaho nia nia

He died like the sun
And the witch climbed up to the top of a pine
Listened 'til evening
To the rumor of the great winds swallowed in the phial
And the lying skalds have sworn to this
Mai Mai ramaho nia nia

▪

Croniamantal was quiet for a second, then added: "I'll never again write any poetry but one free of all shackles, even that of language.

"Listen old buddy!

MAHEVIDANOMI RENANOCALIPNODITOC
EXTARTINAP + V.S.
A.Z.
Tel.: 33-122 Bang:Bang
OeaoiiiioKTin
iiiiiiiiiiii"

"Your last line, my poor Croniamantal," said the Bird of Benin, "is a direct plagiarism of Fr.nc.s J.mm.s."

"That's not true," said Croniamantal. "But I'll write no more poetry. Look what's happened to me because of you. I want to write for the theater."

"You'd do better to go see the girl I told you about. She knows you and seems crazy about you. You'll find her in the Bois de Meudon next Thursday. I'll tell you where. You'll recognize her by the jump rope she'll be holding. Her name is Tristouse Ballerinette."

"Good," said Croniamantal, "I'll go see Ballerinette and sleep with her, but first I want to go to The Theaters to take my play *Ieximal Jelimite*, which I wrote in your studio last year while eating lemons."

"Do whatever you want, my friend," said the Bird of Benin, "but don't forget Tristouse Ballerinette, your future woman."

"Well said," said Croniamantal, "but I want to roar out the plot of *Ieximal Jelimite* one more time. Listen:

"A man buys a newspaper on the seashore. From a house on the prompt-side comes a soldier whose hands are light bulbs. A ten-foot-tall giant jumps down from a tree. He shakes the newsboy, who is plaster and falls down and breaks. Just then a judge pops in. He kills everyone with a razor, while a leg comes hopping along and brains the judge by kicking him under the nose, and sings a pretty little song."

"Marvelous!" said the Bird of Benin, "I'll do the sets. You promised."

"It goes without saying," replied Croniamantal.

11. *Dramaturgy*

The next day Croniamantal went to The Theaters, which were meeting at Mr. Pingu's, the financier. Croniamantal managed to have himself introduced by greasing the palms of the ticket-taker and the fireman. He fearlessly walked into the hall where The Theaters, their acolytes, hired killers, and lackeys were gathered.

CRONIAMANTAL

Gentleman of The Theaters, I've come to read you my play *Ieximal Jelimite*.

THE THEATERS

Please, wait just a moment sir, until we acquaint you with our usages. Here you are among us, our actors, our authors, our critics, and our spectators. Listen carefully and talk very little.

CRONIAMANTAL

I thank you, sirs, for the cordial welcome you are giving me, and I'm sure I'll profit from what you have to say.

THE ACTOR

My roles lasted as last the roses
But mother I love my metempsychoses
O seals of Proteus and his metamorphoses

AN OLD STAGE MANAGER

You remember, madam! One snowy evening in 1832, a lost stranger knocked on the door of a villa located on the road from Chanteboun to Sorrento. . . .

THE CRITIC

For a play to succeed, nowadays, it's important that it not be signed by its author.

THE TRAINER TO HIS BEAR

Now roll over in the peas
Play dead. . . . Give suck. . . .
Dance the polka . . . now the mazurka. . . .

CHORUS OF DRINKERS

Juice of the vine
Rosy wine
Let's drink drink
Until we sink

CHORUS OF EATERS

We're such hogs
That we eat
Even the dogs
At our feet

DRINKERS

Faces flushed with wine
Let's drink drink
The product of the vine

R.D..RD K.PL.NG, ACTOR, ACTRESS, AUTHORS

(*to the Spectators*)

Pay! Pay! Pay! Pay! Pay! Pay! Pay!

THE PREACHER

The Theater, brethren, is a school for scandal. It's a place of perdition for the body and soul. Witness the stagehands: they say all is deceit in the theater. Witches older than Morgan manage to pass themselves off as fifteen-year-old girls.

How much blood is spilled in a melodrama! I tell you truly, though this blood be false, it will fall by proxy on the heads of the children of the authors, the actors, the directors, and the spectators, unto the seventh generation. *Ne mater suam*, girls used to say to their mothers. Today they ask, "Are we going to the theater tonight?"

I tell you truly, brethren. There are few spectacles that do not put the soul in danger. Outside of the spectacle of nature, I know of only one place you can go fearlessly, and that is the farter's booth. This spectacle, brethren, is Gallic and healthy. The sound is a gut-buster; it chases Satan from the loins where he lies; and that's how the Holy Fathers of the desert manage to exorcise themselves from the inside.

AN ACTRESS' MOTHER

Did you f . . . , Charlotte?

THE ACTRESS

No, mother, I'm belching.

MR. MAURICE BOISSARD

Now there you have the guts of today's mother!

AN AUTHOR WHO HAS A PLAY ACCEPTED BY THE COMÉDIE-FRANÇAISE

My friend, you don't seem to be broken in yet. I'm going to teach you the meanings of a few words in the theatrical vocabulary. Listen closely and remember them if you can.

Acheron (hard ch or simply raise hell ad libitum): River of Hades and not hell.

Artists (two types): Is used only when speaking of an actor or actress.

Brother: Avoid modifying this noun with the qualificative "little." The adjective "young" is more suitable.

Nota Bene: This remark does not apply to the operetta.

High-life: This very French expression is translated into English by "fashionable people."

Acquaintances: They are always dangerous in the theater.

Nōh: Is not "no."

Cooked potatoes (is not used in the singular): A raw vegetable detrimental to the stomach.

Damn: This already outdated word advantageously replaced the four-letter word "shit" twenty years ago.

Would you also like some titles? They are important for success.

Here are some sure things:

A SENSE OF POWER; *The Bower;* THINGS GO SOUR; *The Tower;* EAT A FLOWER; *Louise, your shirt is not clean;* HASTEN SLOWLY; *The Tentacular Bar;* FIFTIENTH ON YOUR LEFT; *The Sorceress;* THE GUELPH; *I'm going to kill you;* MY PRINCE; *The Artichoke;* SCHOOL FOR NOTARIES; *The Torchbearer.*

Good-bye, sir, please do not thank me.

A GREAT CRITIC

Gentlemen, I have come to submit to you my account of last night's triumph. Are you ready? I begin:

THE FIST AND THE FRISK

Play in three acts by Julien Meanwhile, Jean de la Slot, Prosper Mordus, and Mrs. Natalie de l'Angoumois, Jane Fountain, and the Countess des Ponds. Decor by Alfred Mone, Leon Minie, Al. de Lemere. Costumes by Jeannette, hats by Wilhelmina, furniture from MacTead's, phonographs from the House of Hernstein, hygienic napkins from Van Feuler and Co.

One recalls the captive who dared f . . . in front of Sesostris. I knew of no more frisky situation before seeing the play by etc. I'm speaking of the scene which came off beautifully on opening night and in which Prominoff, the financier, protests before the examining magistrate.

The play, which is good, has not, however, given all that one expected. The married courtesan, who cooks up a scheme whereby she gets plenty of lettuce from the green old age of a home-brewer, remains nonetheless an unforgettable figure who leaves Cleopatra and Madame de Pompadour far behind. Mr. Layol is a good comic; he impresses us as Familyman in every sense of the word. Miss Jeanine Thehole, a young star of tomorrow, has very pretty legs. But the revelation was Madame Gumshoe, whose sensitive heart was known to all. She mimed the reconciliation scene with the most moving temperament. All in all, a lovely evening from this play which should have a long run.

THE THEATERS

Young man, we're going to tell you a few subjects for plays. If they were signed by known names we'd play them, but these are masterpieces by unknowns which have been entrusted to us and which, because you are a personable young man, we are about to bestow upon you.

Problem Play: The Prince of San Meco finds a louse on his wife's head. He brushes it off and makes a scene. For six months the princess has slept with no one but the Viscount of Dendelope. The spouse makes a scene with the Viscount who, having slept only with the princess and Madame Lafoulue, the wife of a Secretary of State, has the government overthrown and overwhelms Madame Lafoulue with his scorn.

Madame Lafoulue makes a scene with her husband. Everything is explained when Mister Bibier, the Senator, arrives. He scratches his head. He is deloused. He accuses his voters of being lousy. Finally everything is resolved.

Title: "Parliamentary Procedure."

Character Piece: Isabelle Daddy-Longlegs promises her husband to be faithful to him. Then she remembers having promised the same thing to Jules, the shopboy. She suffers from being unable to reconcile her good faith and her love.

Meanwhile, Longlegs fires Jules. This event determines the triumph of love and we find that Isabelle has become a cashier in a big store where Jules works.

Title: "Isabelle Daddy-Longlegs"

Historical Play: The famous novelist Stendhal is at the center of a Bonapartist plot which is ended by the heroic death of a young singer during a presentation of *Don Juan* at la Scala in Milan. Since Stendhal goes under a pseudonym, he gets out of the affair admirably. Grand processions, historical characters.

Opera: The ass of Buridan is hesitant about satisfying his hunger and thirst. The she-ass of Balaam prophecies that the ass will die. The golden ass comes in, eats and drinks. Donkey Skin shows her nudity to this asinine bunch. While passing through, the ass of Sancho, pensive, decides to prove his robustness by kidnapping the Infanta, but the traitorous Melo warns the Genius of La Fontaine. He proclaims his jealousy and kicks the golden ass. Metamorphoses. The Prince and the Infanta enter on horses. The King abdicates in their favor.

Patriotic Play: The Mexican government brings suit against France for counterfeiting Mexican jumping beans. In the last act, they exhume the remains of a fourteenth-century alchemist who invented these beans at La Ferté-Gaucher.

Vaudeville:

A driver who was quite appealing
Yelled to the lady next door:

If you let me see your ceiling
I'll let you see my floor.

Here sir, is enough to nourish an entire life of dramaturgy.

MR. LACOUFF, ERUDITE

Young man, it's also important to know a few theatrical anecdotes, since they agreeably nourish the conversation of a young dramatic author. Here are a few:

Frederick the Great was in the habit of having actresses whipped. He felt that flagellation lent a pink to their skin, which is not without charm.

At the court of the Grand Turk, the *Would-Be Gentleman* was performed, but adapted to local tastes. There Mamamouchi became a knight of the Order of the Garter.

Cecille Vestris, on her way to Mayence one day, saw her coach stopped by the famous Rhenish brigand Schinderhannes. But she kept her chin up and even danced for Schinderhannes in an inn.

Ibsen once slept with a young Spanish girl who cried out at the right moment: "Now! . . . Now! . . . Playwright!"

An erudite actor told me he liked only one statue: *Squatting Scribe*, sculpted by an Egyptian, long before Jesus Christ, and which is in the Louvre. . . . But Mr. Scribe is mentioned less and less these days. Nevertheless, he still reigns over the theater.

THE THEATERS

Don't forget the big scene, nor the curtain line, nor that the more you flop the more you shine, nor that any number cited should end with a seven or a three in order to seem likely, nor never to lend money to anyone who says, "I've got a five-acter at the Odéon," or "I've got a three-acter at the Comédie-Française," nor to say negligently: "If you'd like some free passes, I have so many that I have to give them to my concierge."

Just then a young man came in to sing curious songs with lascivious, silly, and stirring tunes which he sang with ambiguous gestures.

MR. PINGU

What stuff, sir, what stuff!

MR. LACOUFF

Hot what?

MR. PINGU
No, I mean, what sauce!
He jiggles like the belly of an archbishop!

MR. LACOUFF
Employ the proper word—we don't mean the belly.

MR. PINGU
He's really hot stuff! Why, he'd make a crocodile weep, soften a scholar's heart, even a financier's!

CRONIAMANTAL
Gentlemen, good-bye. I am your humble servant. And with your permission, I shall return in a few days. I have the idea that my play is not quite right yet.

12. *Love*

That spring morning, Croniamantal, following what the little Bird of Benin had told him, came to the Bois de Meudon and stretched out in the shade of a tree with very low branches.

CRONIAMANTAL
God! I'm tired, not of walking, but of being alone. I'm thirsty, not for wine, or hydromel, or cervesia, but water, cool water in this pretty wood where the grass and trees are covered with dew each morning, but where no spring stops the thirsty traveler. The walk made me hollow as a gourd. I'm hungry, not for meat or fruit, but bread, good bread, kneaded and swollen like breasts, bread round as the moon and golden brown like it.

He got up. Then he plunged into the woods and came out in the clearing where he was to meet Tristouse Ballerinette. The damsel hadn't come yet, and, having wished for a spring, Croniamantal's will, or rather his diviner's talent (of which he was unaware) caused a clear stream to gush forth and flow out over the grass.

Croniamantal fell to his knees and drank greedily, while a woman's voice sang in the distance:

Dondidondaine
The shepherdess loved by the king

She went to the fountain
Dondidondaine
Through the damp fields turning green
At the fountain
Will he come or will he not?
Here comes Boogyman
To the fountain
Don't tra-la move la-lot.

CRONIAMANTAL

Are you already thinking of her who sings? You laugh feebly at this clearing. Do you think it has been rounded off like a round table for the equality of men and weeks? No! Croniamantal. You know the days are unlike one another.

Around the round table the brave are not equal: one has the sunlight in his face, it dazzles him and soon leaves him to dazzle his neighbor while still another has his own shadow before him. All of them are brave as you yourself are brave, but they are no more equal than night and day.

THE VOICE

Boogyman
Brings roses and thyme
The king comes along—Hello, Germaine
Boogyman
You'll come back some other time

CRONIAMANTAL

Women's voices are always ironic. Is the weather always so beautiful? Someone is already damned in my place. It's nice here in the deep woods. Don't listen to the woman's voice. Ask! Ask!

THE VOICE

—Hello Germaine,
I come to lie with you
—Ah! Sire our cow is full again
—Really Germaine
—And ah! your servant too

CRONIAMANTAL

She who sings to draw me near will be as unknowing as I and dancing wearily.

THE VOICE

The cow is full again
When autumn came she calved
Good-bye my king Dondidondaine
The cow is full again
Alone my heart is broken in half

Croniamantal stood on tiptoe, peering through the branches, to see if he couldn't see her coming, she whom he wanted so much.

THE VOICE

Dondidondaine
It's so cold at the spring
But come Boogyman
Dondidondaine
It'll be less cold come spring

A young girl, dark and svelte, appeared in the clearing. Her face was somber and starred with shifting eyes like birds with bright feathers. Her neck was left bare by her short, dishevelled hair, which was thick and black like a forest at night, and by the jump rope she was holding, Croniamantal recognized Tristouse Ballerinette.

CRONIAMANTAL

Go no further, girl with bare arms. I myself will come toward you. Someone is hiding behind the whitethorn and might hear us.

TRISTOUSE

He who came from an egg like a Tyndaride. I remember that my mother, who is a simple woman, tells me about him sometimes on long evenings. He who looks for snake's eggs is the son of a snake himself. I'm afraid of these old memories.

CRONIAMANTAL

Have no fear, girl with bare arms.

Stay with me. My lips are full of kisses. Here, here. I put them on your forehead, on your hair. I bite your hair with its ancient perfume. I bite your hair which coils like worms on the body of death.

O death, O hairy, wormy death. My lips are full of kisses. Here,

here, on your hands, on your neck, on your eyes, on your eyes, on your eyes. My lips are full of kisses, here, here, burning like fever, pressed to bewitch you, kisses, mad kisses, on the ear, on the temple, on the cheek. Feel my embrace, bend under the strength of my arms, be weary, be weary, be weary. My lips are full of kisses, here, here, mad, on your neck, on your hair, on your forehead, on your eyes, on your mouth. O how I want to love you on this spring day when there are no longer blossoms on the branches beginning to bear fruit.

TRISTOUSE

Leave me alone, go away, those who love one another are happy, but I don't love you. You frighten me. And yet, do not despair, O poet. Listen, this is my best proverb: Go away.

CRONIAMANTAL

Alas! Alas! To leave again, to go until the ocean stops me, across the heaths, the fir plantations, in the peat, the mud, and the dust, across the forests and the meadows, through the orchards and the blissful gardens.

TRISTOUSE

Go away. Go far away from the ancient smell of my hair, O you who belong to me.

And Croniamantal went away without looking back; for a long time he could be seen through the branches, then, when he had disappeared, his voice kept going further away, diminishing.

CRONIAMANTAL

A poet without a pen, an editor without a staff, a traveler without a walking stick, a pilgrim without a bourdon, I am the weakest of all men, I have nothing left and I know nothing.

And his voice no longer came as far as Tristouse Ballerinette, who was looking at herself in the spring.

In other times, some of the monks were clearing the Malvern Forest.

MONKS

The sun goes down slowly, and giving thanks to Thee, Lord, we are going back to the monastery to sleep, so the dawn will find us in the forest once again.

MALVERN FOREST

Every day, every day, bewildered flights of crazed birds see their nests crushed and eggs broken when the trees come crashing down, shaking their limbs.

THE BIRDS

It is the joyous moment of dusk when girls and boys come to frolic on the green. And all have kisses that are ready to fall like overripe fruit or like the egg when it is about to be laid. See them, see them dancing, dawdling, haunting, singing from the blue dusk until dawn, his white sister.

A RED-HEADED MONK, *in the cortege*

I'm afraid of living and I would die. Tremblings of the earth! Work, O lost time . . .

THE BIRDS

Ho heigh the broken egg
The ready-made omelet cooked on a lightning bug
Here here
Go right
Turn left
Down low in the air
Like a broken kite
There and there

CRONIAMANTAL, *in another time and near the Malvern Forest, a little before the passing of the monks*

Winds part in front of me, forests fall away to become a wide way, with rotting corpses here and there. Travelers have encountered too many corpses for some time now, chattering, rotting corpses.

THE RED-HEADED MONK

I don't want to work any more, I want to dream and pray.

He lay down, his face turned toward the sky, in the road lined with fog-colored willows.

Night had come with its moonlight. Croniamantal saw the monks bent over the listless body of their brother. Then he heard a low mourning, a weak outcry that died in a last sigh. And they passed slowly in single file in front of Croniamantal, hidden behind a clump of willows.

THE GLORIDE FOREST

I'd like to mislead this man among the ghosts that float among the birches. But he escapes toward the time to come and now he's there.

A banging of distant doors changed into the sound of a moving train. A wide road, grassy, crossed with trunks, edged with large rocks. Life commits suicide. A path people run down. They never get tired. Tunnels where the air is foul. Cadavers. Voices call Croniamantal, he runs, he runs, he descends.

▪

In the pretty woods, Tristouse was strolling along, meditating.

TRISTOUSE

My heart is sad without you, Croniamantal. I loved you without knowing it. Everything is green. Everything is green above my head and below my feet. I've lost the one I loved. I'll have to look here and there, about and everywhere. And among the many, many, there should be someone who will please me.

Come back from other times, Croniamantal, before noticing Tristouse and on seeing the spring again, cried out:

CRONIAMANTAL

Divinity! Which are you? Where is your eternal form?

TRISTOUSE

There he is handsomer than before and any. . . . Listen, O poet, I am yours from now on.

Without looking at Tristouse, Croniamantal leaned over the spring.

CRONIAMANTAL

I love springs, they are a beautiful symbol of immortality when they do not run dry. This one has never run dry. And I seek a divinity, but I want her to seem eternal. And my spring has never run dry.

He got down on his knees and prayed before the spring as Tristouse, all in tears, lamented.

TRISTOUSE

O poet, do you adore the spring? O my God, give me back my lover! Come! I know such beautiful songs.

CRONIAMANTAL

The spring has its murmur.

TRISTOUSE

Well then, sleep with your cold lover! I hope she drowns you. But if you live, you belong to me and you will obey me.

She went away, and across the forest with its twittering birds, the spring ran on and murmured, while Croniamantal's voice rose as he wept and his tears mixed with the beloved water.

CRONIAMANTAL

O spring! You who spring forth like inexhaustible blood. You who are as cold as marble, but living, transparent, and fluid. You who are always new and always the same. You who quicken your banks turning green, I adore you. You are my incomparable divinity. You will refresh me. You will purify me. You'll murmur your eternal song to me and you'll put me to sleep in the evening.

THE SPRING

Down in my little bed filled with an Orient of gems, I hear you with pleasure, O poet! whom I have enchanted. I remember an Avalon where we could have lived, you as the Fisher King and I awaiting you under the apple trees. O island of apple trees! But I am happy in my priceless little bed. These amethysts are sweet to look upon. This lapis lazuli is bluer than a blue sky. This malachite makes me think of a meadow. Sardonyx, onyx, agate, rock crystal, you'll shine tonight. Because I want to give a feast in honor of my lover. I'll come alone, as befits a virgin. The power of my lover the poet is already manifest and his presents are dear to my heart. He has given me his eyes all in tears, two adorable springs, tributaries of my stream.

CRONIAMANTAL

O fertile spring, your water seems your hair. Flowers are born around you, and we will love each other forever.

All that was heard were the songs of the birds and rustling of leaves, and sometimes the splashing of a bird playing in the water.

A fonipoit appeared in the little wood: it was Paponat the Algerian. He came dancing toward the spring.

CRONIAMANTAL

I know you. You are Paponat, who studied in the East.

PAPONAT

In person. O poet of the West, I come to visit you. I learned of your conversion, but I understand there is still a way of conversing with you. The humidity! It's not surprising your voice is raucous—you'll need a calcophane to clear it up. I came dancing up to you. Would there be any way of getting you out of this situation?

CRONIAMANTAL

Phooey! But tell me who taught you to dance.

PAPONAT

The very angels were my dancing masters.

CRONIAMANTAL

The good angels or the bad ones? What does it matter, I'm not insisting. I'm tired of all dances except for one I'd like to be able to do again, the one the Greeks called *kordax*.

PAPONAT

You're gay, Croniamantal, we're going to have a good time. I'm glad I came. I love gaiety! I'm happy!

And Paponat, his eyes shining, deep, and swirling, laughed, rubbing his hands together.

CRONIAMANTAL

You look like me!

PAPONAT

Hardly. I'm happy to be alive and you're dying near the spring.

CRONIAMANTAL

But this happiness you proclaim, are you forgetting it? And mine? You look like me! The happy man rubs his hands together, as you did. Smell them. How do they smell?

PAPONAT

Like death.

CRONIAMANTAL
Ha! ha! ha! The happy man smells just like death. Rub your hands together. Some difference between a happy man and a cadaver! I'm happy too, though I don't want to rub my hands together. Be happy, rub your hands together. Be happy! More! Now do you know it, the smell of happiness?

PAPONAT
Adieu, if you make no case for the living anymore, there's no way of talking to you.

And while Paponat went off into the night where shine the innumerable eyes of the celestial animals of impalpable flesh, Croniamantal suddenly stood up and thought:

"That's enough of nature and the memories it evokes. Now I know enough about life, let's go back to Paris and try to find that exquisite Tristouse Ballerinette who loves me madly."

13. *Fashion*

The fonipoit Paponat, who at night was returning from the Bois de Meudon, where he had been in search of adventure, arrived just in time to take the last boat. There he had the good fortune to encounter Tristouse Ballerinette.

"How are you, miss?" he said to her. "In the Bois de Meudon I encountered your lover, Monsieur Croniamantal, who is in the process of going mad."

"My lover?" said Tristouse. "He is not my lover."

"Still, that's what they're saying, since last night, in our literary and artistic circles."

"They can say what they want," said Tristouse firmly. "Besides, there's no reason to blush about having him for a lover. Isn't he handsome? And doesn't he have great talent?"

"You're right. But my what a lovely dress! And your hat! I'm very interested in fashion."

"You are always very elegant, Mister Paponat. Give me your tailor's address. I'll tell Croniamantal about him."

"Useless, he wouldn't go," said Paponat, laughing. "But tell me:

what are the ladies wearing this year? I've just arrived from Italy and I'm not up to date. Please tell me about it."

"This year," said Tristouse, "fashions are bizarre and common, simple and full of fantasy. Any material from nature's domain can now be introduced into the composition of women's clothes. I saw a charming dress made of corks. It was certainly equal to the charming washcloth evening dresses which are the rage at the premieres. A big designer is thinking about launching tailor-made outfits made of old bookbindings done in calf. It's charming. All the ladies of letters would want to wear them, and one could approach them and whisper in their ear under the pretext of reading the titles. Fish bones are being worn a lot on hats. One often sees delicious young girls dressed like pilgrims of Saint James of Compostella; their outfits, as is fitting, are studded with coquilles Saint-Jacques. Steel, wool, sandstone, and the file have made an abrupt entry into the vestmentary arts. These materials are used in belts, on hat pins, etc; and it so happened that I saw an adorable reticule composed entirely of glass eyes, the kind you see at the oculists'. Feathers now decorate not only hats, but shoes, gloves, and next year they'll be on umbrellas. They're doing shoes in Venetian glass and hats in Baccarat crystal. Not to mention oil-painted dresses, brightly colored wools, or dresses curiously splashed with ink. For spring wear, there'll be many clothes made of bladders, pleasant shapes, light and distinctive. Our lady fliers will wear nothing else. For the races, there will be the child's balloon hat, made of around twenty balloons, a very luxurious effect and sometimes some diverting detonations. The mussel shell is worn only on high-top shoes. Notice that they're beginning to dress in live animals. I encountered one lady whose hat had twenty birds: canaries, goldfinches, robins, held with a wire on the claw, singing wildly and flapping their wings. The coiffure of an ambassadress was, at the last party in Neuilly, composed of thirty snakes. 'For whom are these serpents which hiss on your head?' said a little Roumanian attaché with the Dacian accent, who has the reputation of being successful with women. I forgot to tell you that last Wednesday I saw on the boulevards an old dowager dressed in mirrors stuck to fabric. The effect was sumptuous in the sunlight. You'd have thought it was a gold mine out for a walk. Later it started raining and the lady looked like a silver mine. Nut shells make pretty trimmings, especially if they're mixed with hazelnuts. Dresses embellished with coffee beans, cloves, cloves of garlic, onions, and bunches of raisins, these will be perfect for social calls. Fashion is becoming practical and no longer looks down on anything. It ennobles everything. It does for materials what the Romantics did for words."

"Thank you," said Paponat, "you have informed me most charmingly."

"You are too nice," replied Tristouse.

14. *Meetings*

Six months passed. For the last five of them Tristouse Ballerinette had been Croniamantal's mistress, and she loved him passionately for a week. In exchange for this love, the lyrical boy had made her immortal and glorious forever by celebrating her in marvelous poems.

"I was unknown," she thought, "and now he's made me illustrious among all living women.

"They used to think I was generally ugly with my thinness, my oversized mouth, my horrible teeth, my asymmetrical face, and my crooked nose. But now I'm beautiful and all the men tell me so. They used to make fun of my manly, jerky walk, my pointed elbows moving like chicken legs. Now I'm considered so gracious the other women imitate me.

"What miracles a poet's love can give birth to! But it weighs heavily, this poets'-love! What sadness comes with it, what silences to undergo! But now the miracle is done, I'm beautiful and glorious. Croniamantal is ugly and in no time he's run through his money; he's poor and lacking in grace, he's dull, and his least gesture makes him a hundred enemies.

"I don't love him anymore, I don't love him anymore.

"I don't need him anymore, my admirers are enough. I'll break off slowly. But the slow method will be a bother. I've got to leave, or he has to leave, so he won't give me any trouble, so he won't blame me for anything."

And, after a week, Tristouse became Paponat's mistress, while still seeing Croniamantal, with whom she was colder and colder. She went to see him less and less and he felt worse and worse, but he grew fonder and fonder of Tristouse, being happy only when she was there, and, on the days she didn't come, he spent hours in front of the house where she lived, hoping to see her come out, and if by chance she appeared, he ran away like a thief, for fear that she'd accuse him of spying on her.

▪

It was while running after Tristouse Ballerinette like this that Croniamantal continued his literary education.

One day when he was trudging across Paris he suddenly found himself beside the Seine. He passed over a bridge and walked a little further when suddenly, noticing Mr. François Coppée ahead of him, Croniamantal regretted that this stroller was dead. But nothing prevents you from talking to a dead person, and the meeting was pleasant.

"You've got to admit," thought Croniamantal, "for a stroller, he's quite a stroller, in fact the very author of *The Stroller*. He's a skillful and witty rhymer full of a feeling for reality. Why not talk with him about rhyme?"

The poet of *The Stroller* was smoking a black cigarette. He was dressed in black, his face was black; he was funnily standing on a block of stone, and Croniamantal could clearly see by his pensive air that he was working on a poem. Croniamantal approached him, and after saying hello he said point-blank:

"Dear master, you look so somber."

He replied courteously:

"It's because my statue is bronze. It exposes me to constant mistakes. Thus, the other day,

Strolling by me the Negro Sam MacVea
Saw me blacker than he and wept at the idea

"See how clever these lines are. I'm in the process of perfecting rhyme. Have you noticed that the distich I recited for you rhymes perfectly for the eye."

"Yes," said Croniamantal, "because it's pronounced *Sam MacVea*, as in *Shakespeer*."

"Here's something that will do the job better," continued the statue:

"Strolling by me the Negro Sam MacVea
Wrote three names on the base immediately

Now there is a seductive refinement, the full rhyme for the ear."

"You enlighten me on the subject of rhyme," said Croniamantal. "And I'm very happy, my dear master, to have strolled your way."

"It's my first success," replied the metallic poet. "However, I have just composed a little poem bearing the same title: there is a man walking along, *The Stroller*, down the corridor of a railroad coach; he spies a charming lady with whom he stops at the Dutch frontier instead of going straight on to Brussels.

They passed at least a month at Rosendeal
He liked the ideal she loved the real
In every way he was different from her
Thus it was love that they knew there

"I call your attention to these last two lines; although rich in rhyme, they contain a dissonance which causes a delicate contrast between the full sound of masculine rhymes and the morbidity of the feminine ones."

"Dear master," said Croniamantal louder, "tell me about free verse."

"Long live freedom!" cried the bronze statue.

And after tipping his hat, Croniamantal went on, hoping to meet Tristouse.

▪

Another day, Croniamantal was walking along the boulevards. Tristouse had not come to a rendezvous and he was hoping to run into her at a fashionable tea shop where she sometimes went with friends. He was turning the corner of the rue Le Peletier when a gentleman wearing a pearl-gray cape approached him saying:

"Sir, I am going to reform letters. I have found a sublime subject: it consists of the sensations experienced by a polite young man who lets an unspeakable noise escape in a gathering of ladies and girls of quality."

Croniamantal, astonished by the novelty of the subject, immediately understood how it lent itself to enhancing the author's sensibility.

Croniamantal left. . . . A lady stepped on his toes. She was an author and didn't lose the opportunity to state that this encounter or collision would furnish her with a subject for a delicate short story.

Croniamantal took to his heels and ended up near the Pont des

Saints-Pères, where three people discussing the subject of a novel asked him to judge their case; it was a question of writing the story of a hero.

"Fine subject!" exclaimed Croniamantal.

"Wait," said the man next to him, a bearded man. "I think the subject is still too new and too odd for the current public."

And the third man explained that it concerned a hero sandwich. . . .

But Croniamantal didn't answer, he was off to visit an old cook who wrote poetry. He hoped to see Tristouse there at teatime. Tristouse wasn't there, but Croniamantal chatted with the mistress of the house, who recited a few poems for him.

It was a poetry full of depth where all the words had new meanings. Thus, she used *archipelago* only in the sense of *blotter*.

▪

A little later, the rich Paponat, proud of being able to call himself the lover of the famous Tristouse, and who did not want to lose her, because she did him honor, decided to take his mistress on a trip across central Europe.

"All right," said Tristouse, "but we will not travel as lovers, because although I think you're nice, I don't love you or at least I try not to. So we'll travel as buddies. I'll dress like a boy; my hair is not long and I've often been told that I look like a handsome young man."

"O.K.," said Paponat, "and since you need some rest and I too am a bit worn out, we'll go on retreat in Moravia, in a convent at Brunn where my uncle, the prior of Crépontois, retired after the expulsion of the monks. It's one of the richest and most pleasant convents in the world. I'll introduce you as one of my friends and, have no fear, we'll pass for lovers just the same."

"That'll be fine," said Tristouse, "because I adore passing for something I'm not. We leave tomorrow."

15. *Travel*

Losing Tristouse, Croniamantal went sort of crazy. But at that point he was becoming famous, and as his reputation as a poet grew, his vogue as a dramatist grew also.

The theaters performed his plays and the crowd applauded his name, but at the same time the enemies of poets and poetry were increasing and their bold hatred was growing.

He was sadder and sadder. His soul was becoming rarified in his powerless body.

When he learned that Tristouse had gone away, he took it calmly, but asked the concierge if she knew the purpose of the trip.

"I don't know about that," the woman said. "All I know is she's gone to central Europe."

"Good," said Croniamantal.

Back at his place, he got together his several thousand francs and at the Gare du Nord took the train for Germany.

▪

And the next day, Christmas Eve, on schedule, the train was engulfed in the enormous station of Cologne. Croniamantal, a little suitcase in his hand, was the last to come out of his third-class coach. On the platform parallel to his, the stationmaster's red cap, the spherical helmets of the police, and the top hats of notables indicated that someone of importance was expected on the next train. And in fact, Croniamantal heard a little old man who was gesturing curtly and whose fat, astonished wife was gaping at the red cap, the spherical helmets, and the top hats:

"Krupp . . . Essen . . . No orders . . . Italy."

Croniamantal followed the crowd of travelers brought in on his train. He was walking behind two girls for whom it must have been "back door," so much did they walk like geese. They concealed their hands under short capes; the head of the first was decorated with a minuscule black hat on which were stuck bunches of blue roses, while straight black feathers, whose spines were plucked clean except at the tips, shivered above as if from cold. The hat of the second girl was of smooth, almost brilliant, felt: an enormous bow of violet sateen overshadowed it ludicrously. They were probably two maids out of work, because as they were passing by they were snapped up, so to speak, by a group of bedecked and ugly ladies wearing the ribbons of the Catholic Society for the Protection of Girls. The ladies of the Protestant Society, who performed the same function, were stationed further along. Croniamantal, now behind a large man with a hard, short, reddish beard, dressed in green, went down the stairway that leads to the station's entrance hall.

Outside, he greeted the solitary Dome in the center of the irregular square it fills with its mass. The station jammed its own modern mass in near the immense cathedral. Hotels displayed their signs in hybrid language and, though near the Gothic colossus, seemed to keep a respectful distance. For a long time Croniamantal sniffed the town's air in front of the cathedral. He seemed disappointed.

"She's not here," he said to himself. "My nose would smell her, my nerves would vibrate, my eyes would see her."

He walked through town, passed the fortifications as if he were being driven by an unknown force down the highway, downstream, on the right bank of the Rhine. And in fact, Tristouse and Paponat had arrived the night before in Cologne, bought a car, and were continuing their trip, following the right bank of the Rhine in the direction of Coblenz, and Croniamantal was hot on their trail.

▪

Christmas night arrived. A prophetic old rabbi from Dollendorf, the moment he set foot on the bridge that links Bonn to Beul, was pushed back by a violent gust of wind. The snow was blowing furiously. The noise of the storm drowned out the Christmas carols, but the thousand lights on the trees were sparkling in every house.

The old Jew swore:

"*Kreuzdonnerwetter* . . . I'll never get to *Haenchen*. . . . Winter, old friend, you can't hurt my joyous old carcass, so let me cross this old Rhine which is drunk as umpteen drunkards. Me, the only reason I'm on my way to the noble tavern frequented by Borussians is to get stewed in the company of those white caps and at their expense, like a good Christian, though I am a Jew."

The storm's noise redoubled. Strange voices were heard. The old rabbi shivered and looked up at the sky yelling:

"Donnerkeil! Ui jeh! ch, ch, ch. Eh! hey up there, you ought to tend to your own knitting instead of bothering the joyous buggers whose fate makes them be out walking on a night like this. . . . Eh! mothers, are you no longer under Solomon's rule? Ohe! Ohe! Tseilom Kop! Meicabl! Farwaschen Ponim! Beheime! You're trying to keep me from drinking the excellent Moselle with the Borussian students who are more than glad to clink glasses with me because of my famous learning and my inimitable lyricism, not counting all my gifts for sorcery and prophecy.

"Damned spirits! Know that I would have had some Rhine wines too, as well as the wines of France. And I wouldn't have forgotten to soak up a little champagne in your honor, my old friends. . . . At midnight, at the hour of *Christkindchen*, I'd have rolled under the table and slept at least through the whole bash. . . . But you unleash the winds, you raise holy hell on this angelic night which should be peaceful. You are aware that we are in the period of halcyon days . . . and, as for quiet, you sound like you're pulling each other's hair out up there, lovely ladies. . . . To amuse Solomon, no doubt. . . . Herrgottsocra . . . what's that? . . . Lilith! Naama! Aguereth! Mahala! . . . Ah! Solomon, for your pleasure they're going to kill every poet on this earth.

"Ah! Solomon! Solomon! jovial king whose entertainers are these four noctural ghosts going from East to North, you want me dead, because I'm a poet too like all the Jewish prophets and a prophet like all the poets.

"Good-bye, drunkenness of this evening . . . I must turn away from you, old Rhine. I'm going to go get ready to die while dictating my last and most lyrical prophecies. . . ."

A sudden crashing, like thunder, broke loose. The old prophet pursed his lips, shook his head, and looked down at the ground, then bent over and pricked up his ears, rather near the ground. When he stood up again he murmured:

"The very Earth can no longer stand its insupportable contact with poets."

Then, he set out through the streets of Beul, away from the Rhine.

When the rabbi had crossed the railroad track, he found himself before two roads and while he hesitated, not knowing which was the right one, he happened to look up again. Ahead of him he saw a young man holding a suitcase and who was coming from Bonn; the old rabbi didn't recognize this person and he yelled out to him.

"You must be crazy to be traveling on a night like this!"

"I'm in a hurry to find someone I lost but whose trail I'm on," replied the stranger.

"What do you do?" yelled the Jew.
"I'm a poet."

The prophet stamped his foot and, as the young man was going away, insulted him disgracefully because of the pity he felt; then he looked down and forgot about the poet, went to look at the signs to figure out which way to go. He walked straight ahead, grumbling.

"Fortunately the wind has died down . . . at least you can walk. . . . At first I thought he was coming to kill me. But no, he'll probably die before I do, this poet, and he's not even Jewish. Well, let's walk fast and joyously to prepare for a glorious death."

The old rabbi picked up his pace; in his long overcoat he resembled a ghost, and some children, who were coming back from Putzchen after the Christmas tree celebration, went past him, screamed from terror, and threw rocks at him a long time after he had disappeared.

▪

And so it was that Croniamantal went through part of Germany and the Austrian Empire; the force that drove him led him across Thuringia, Saxony, Bohemia, Moravia, all the way to Brunn, where he had to stop.

▪

He walked around town the same night he arrived. In the streets lined with old palaces, huge Swiss guards, in breeches and cocked hats, stood in front of the doors. They were leaning on long canes with crystal pommels. Their gold buttons were shining like cats' eyes.

Croniamantal got lost; he wandered around for a while, walking in a poor neighborhood past houses where shadows passed quickly behind bright windows. Officers in long blue overcoats went by. Croniamantal turned around to follow them with his eyes, then went on outside of town, in the night, to contemplate the dark mass of the Spielberg. While he was looking the old State Prison over, he heard footsteps, then saw three monks go past gesturing and talking. Croniamantal ran after them and asked for directions.

"You're French," they said to him. "Come with us."

Croniamantal looked them over and noticed that over their frocks they were wearing very elegant little beige coats. Each had a cane and was topped off with a bowler. On the way, one of the monks said to Croniamantal:

"You're a long way from your hotel, but we'll show you the way if you wish. But, if you'd like, you're certainly welcome at the monastery; you'll be well received, since you're a foreigner, and you can spend the night there."

Croniamantal was glad to accept, saying:

"I'd love to, because are you not my brothers, since I'm a poet?"

They started laughing. The oldest, whose glasses were rimmed with gold and whose belly stuck out like a sore thumb, lifted his arms and cried:

"Poet! Can it be?"

And the two others, both thinner, bent over and hee-hawed, holding their bellies as if they had a cramp.

"Let's be serious now," said the monk with glasses, "we're going to cross a street where Jews live."

In the streets, on every doorstep, old women standing straight as fir trees in a forest were calling and beckoning.

"Let us flee this whoredom," said the fat monk, who was Czech, and whom his companions called Father Karel.

Finally Croniamantal and the monks stopped in front of a big monastery. They rang the bell and the porter came to the door. The two thin monks said good-bye to Croniamantal and he was left alone with Father Karel in a richly furnished parlor.

"My child," said Father Karel, "you happen to be in a unique monastery. The monks that live here are all very fine people. We have former archdukes and even former architects, soldiers, scholars, poets, inventors, a few monks who came from France after the expulsion of the congregations, and a few well-mannered lay guests. All are saints. I, as you see me, with my glasses and big belly, I too am a saint. I'm going to show you your room, where you'll stay until nine o'clock; then you'll hear the dinner bell and I'll come to get you."

Father Karel guided Croniamantal down long corridors. Then

they went up a white marble stairway and, on the third floor, Father Karel opened a door and said:

"Your room."

He showed him the light switch and left.

The room was round, the bed and furnishings round; on the mantle a death's head looked like an old hunk of cheese.

Croniamantal went over to the window, under which stretched the thick darkness of a large monastic garden from which laughter, sighs, cries of joy seemed to rise, as if a thousand couples were embracing there. Then a woman's voice in the garden sang a song Croniamantal had heard before:

Boogyman
Brings roses and thyme
The king comes in
—Hello, Germaine
—Boogyman
You'll come back some other time

And Croniamantal began singing the rest:

—Hello, Germaine
I come to lie with you

Then he waited for Tristouse's voice to finish the couplet.

And men's voices sang here and there strange songs in bass melodies, while the broken voice of an old man quavered:

Vexilla regis prodeunt . . .

At this moment Father Karel came into the room just as a bell began to clang wildly.

"Well, my boy, listening to the sounds of our fine garden? It's filled with memories, this terrestrial paradise. Tycho Brahe once made love there with a pretty Jewish girl who kept saying, 'Chazer,' which is slang for pig. I myself saw a certain archduke amuse himself with a pretty boy whose behind was shaped like a valentine. But come on, let's go eat!"

▪

They came to a still-empty, vast refectory where the poet could examine at leisure the frescoes that covered the walls.

There was Noah, dead drunk and asleep. His son Shem was uncovering his father's nudity, that is, a vine stalk painted cleverly and naively, whose branches served as a genealogical tree of sorts, because it bore the names of the monastery's abbots, painted in red letters on the leaves.

The marriage of Cana showed a Mannekenpis pissing wine in the big barrels, while the bride, at least eight months pregnant, was presenting her keg-like belly to someone who was writing on it, in charcoal: Tokay.

And there were the soldiers of Gideon relieving themselves of horrible diarrhea caused by the water they had drunk.

The long table in the center of the hall, lengthwise, was set with an uncommon sumptuousness. The glasses and decanters were of cut Bohemian crystal, of the finest red crystal, whose decorations were nothing less than glass encrusted with fern, gold, and garnets. The superb silverware was shining on the whiteness of the tablecloth strewn with violets.

The monks entered two by two, hooded, arms crossed on their chests. As they entered they greeted Croniamantal and went to their usual places, while Father Karel told Croniamantal their names and what countries they were from. Soon the table was complete with fifty-six, Croniamantal included. The abbot, an Italian with slanted eyes, said the blessing and the meal began, but Croniamantal waited anxiously for Tristouse.

First they were served a bouillon swimming with little pieces of bird brains and peas . . .

▪

"Our two French guests have just left," said a French monk who had been the prior of Crépontois. "I couldn't keep them from going: my nephew's friend was singing a little while ago in the garden in his fine soprano voice. He almost fainted when he heard someone, inside the convent, pick up the song. My nephew tried in vain to convince his charming friend to stay; they have left and taken the train, because their car wasn't ready. We are to ship it to them by rail. They didn't tell me where they're going, but I think these pious children have business in Marseille. Anyway, I think I heard them mention that town."

White as a sheet, Croniamantal stood up:

"Excuse me, fathers, but I was wrong to accept your hospitality. I must go, please do not ask me why. But I'll always remember the simplicity, the gaiety, and the freedom that reign here. These things are very dear to me, so why, why, alas, can't I enjoy them?"

16. *Persecution*

Back then poetry prizes were handed out every day. Thousands of societies had been founded for this purpose and their members lived off the fat of the land, giving out, on certain dates, the awards to poets. But the twenty-sixth of January was when the largest societies, companies, boards of directors, academies, committees, juries, etc., etc., of the entire world awarded their prizes. On that day were allotted 8,019 poetry awards whose total came up to 50,003,225.75 francs. On the other hand, a taste for poetry was not widespread in any class of any country, and public opinion ran very high against poets, who were considered lazy, useless, etc. That year the twenty-sixth of January passed without incident, but the next day *The Voice*, the big newspaper published in Adelaide (Australia) in French, contained an article by the agro-chemist Horace Tograth (a German, born in Leipzig), whose discoveries and inventions often bordered on the miraculous. The article, entitled "The Laurel," contained a sort of history of the cultivation of the laurel in Judea, Greece, Italy, Africa, and Provence. The author gave advice to those who had laurels in their gardens; he pointed out the numerous uses of the laurel, in foods, in art, in poetry, and its role as a symbol of poetic glory. He then spoke of it in mythology, making allusions to Apollo and to the fable of Daphne. Near the end, Horace Tograth abruptly changed his tone and concluded his article with:

"And so, I tell you verily, this useless tree is still too common, and we have less glorious symbols to which the people attribute the famous savor of the laurel. The laurel takes up too much space on an overpopulated earth—the laurel is unworthy of life. Every one of them takes up the space of two men in the sun. May they be cut down and their leaves be shunned as poison. But of late still the symbol of poetry and literary science, they are today but the symbol of that death-glory which is to glory what death is to life, what the hand of glory is to the key.

"True glory has abandoned poetry for science, philosophy, acrobatics, philanthropy, sociology, etc. All poets are good for today is sponging money they in no way earn since they barely work and most of them (except the songwriters and a few others) have no talent and consequently no excuse. As for those who possess a certain gift, they are even more noxious, because if they make nothing, for nothing, each one makes more noise than a regiment and bombards our ears with his own cursedness. There is no longer any reason for all these people. The prizes they're awarded are stolen from workers, from inventors, from scientists, from philosophers, from acrobats, from philanthropists, from sociologists, etc. The poets must go. Lycurgus banished them from the Republic; we must banish them from the earth. Unless we do, the poets, those lazy bums, will be our princes, and by doing nothing will live off our work, oppress us, mock us. In short, we must get rid of the poetic tyranny as soon as possible.

"If the republics and kings, if the nations do not watch out, the over-privileged race of poets will increase in such proportions and so rapidly that before long no one will want to work, invent, learn, reason, do dangerous things, remedy the ills of mankind, and better our condition.

"We must, then, immediately deal with and heal ourselves of this poetic cancer which is gnawing at humanity."

This article received tremendous attention. It was telegraphed and telephoned everywhere. All the newspapers reprinted it. A few literary papers followed Tograth's article with sarcastic reflections on the scientist; they had a few doubts about his sanity. They laughed at the terror he displayed before the lyric laurel. The average newspapers, on the contrary, set great stock by his warning. They said the article in *The Voice* was inspired.

Horace Tograth's article had been a remarkable pretext, perfect for asserting a hatred for poetry. And the pretext was poetic. The article by the scientist of Adelaide used the appeal of the marvelousness of antiquity, whose memory lies in every well-born man, and it also appealed to the instinct for self-preservation all beings have. That is why nearly all of Tograth's readers were dazzled, appalled, and eager to harm the poets, who, because of the great number of prizes whose beneficiaries they were, were subject to the jealously of all classes of the population. Most of the newspapers concluded by asking the governments to take steps to suppress at least the awards.

That evening, in a later edition of *The Voice*, the agro-chemist Horace Tograth published a new article which, like the first, telegraphed and telephoned everywhere, raised the feelings of the people and governments to fever pitch. The scientist finished with:

"World, choose between your life and poetry; if serious measures are not taken, it's the end of civilization. You will not hesitate. Tomorrow will begin the new era. Poetry will no longer exist. These heavy lyres for old inspirations will be broken. The poets will be massacred."

▪

That night, life was the same in every town on the globe. The ubiquitously telegraphed article had been reprinted in special editions of the local papers which were immediately snatched up. People everywhere shared Tograth's opinion. The politicians went through the streets and mixed with the crowds, stirring them up. Moreover, that night most governments made decisions whose texts, posted as they appeared bit by bit, provoked an indescribable enthusiasm in the streets. France, Italy, Spain, and Portugal were the first to enact laws by which poets living within their borders were to be imprisoned immediately, until further decisions were made. Foreign or absent poets who tried to enter these countries would risk being condemned to death. It was telegraphed that the United States had decided to electrocute any man whose profession as poet was well known. It was also reported that Germany had decreed that poets and prose-poets living in its territories were to remain in their homes until further notice. In fact during the night and the following day all the countries of the world, even those which had only bad minor poets with no lyric gift, took measures against the very name of poet. There were only two exceptions: England and Russia. These improvised laws were put into immediate effect. All poets on French, Italian, Spanish, and Portuguese soil were put in jail the next day, while some literary papers came out with black borders and lamented the new reign of terror. Dispatches arriving at noon announced that Aristenete Southwest, the great Negro poet of Haiti, had been cut into pieces that same morning and devoured by a mob of Negroes and mulattoes crazed with sun and carnage. In Cologne, the Kaiserglocke had rung all night and the next morning; Professor-Doctor Stimmung, author of a medieval epic in forty-eight cantos, had gone out to catch the train for Hanover and had been chased by a band of fanatics who beat him with sticks and yelled: "Death to the poet!"

He had taken refuge in the cathedral and, with a few beadles, was locked in by the unleashed population of Drikkes, Hannes, and Marizibills. The latter were especially outraged; in Low German they invoked the Virgin, Saint Ursula, and the Three Wise Men, besides hitting everyone and elbowing their way through the crowd. Their paternosters and pious appeals were interlarded with admirably base insults for the professor-poet, who particularly owed his reputation to his unisexuality. Forehead on the floor, he was scared to death under the big wooden Saint Christopher. He heard the sounds of the masons walling up the church's every exit, and he prepared himself to die of hunger.

Around two o'clock, a wire reported that a sexton-poet in Naples had seen the blood of Saint January bubbling in the Holy Ampule. The sexton had run outside proclaiming the miracle and hurried down to the port to play hearts. He had won a great deal and had been stabbed in the chest.

Telegrams announcing the arrests of poets poured in all day long. The electrocution of American poets was learned of around four o'clock.

In Paris a few young poets from the Left Bank, spared because of their lack of notoriety, organized a demonstration which left from the Closerie des Lilas for the Conciergerie, where the Prince of Poets had been locked up. The military arrived to disperse the demonstrators. The cavalry charged. The poets drew weapons and defended themselves, but the people, seeing this, joined the fray. The poets were strangled, as well as anyone who tried to help them.

Thus began the persecution which spread rapidly throughout the world. In America, after the famous poets were electrocuted, the Negro songwriters and even many who had never written a song were lynched; then the whites of literary Bohemia were taken care of. It was learned also that Tograth, after personally directing the persecution in Australia, had embarked at Melbourne.

17. *Assassination*

Like Orpheus, all the poets were on the verge of a violent death. Publishing houses everywhere had been ransacked and the books of poetry burned. Massacres had taken place in every town. For the moment universal admiration went to this Horace Tograth, who, from

Adelaide (Australia), had unleashed the storm and seemed to have destroyed poetry forever. This man's knowledge, they said, seemed miraculous. He dispersed clouds or led a storm to wherever he wished. When women saw him they were ready to do whatever he wanted. Besides, he did not disdain a virginity whether feminine or masculine. When Tograth realized the universal enthusiasm he had aroused, he announced that he would visit the principal cities of the globe, after Australia had gotten rid of its erotic or elegiac poets. In fact, a little later it was learned that Tokyo, Peking, Yakutsk, Calcutta, Cairo, Buenos Aires, San Francisco, and Chicago had gone wild when the infamous German Tograth had visited them. He left a supernatural impression everywhere because of his miracles, which he described as scientific, and because of his extraordinary cures which raised his reputation as scientist and miracle worker to the sublime.

On May thirtieth Tograth disembarked at Marseille. The whole town had crowded onto the docks. Tograth came in from the steamer in a launch. When he was sighted, cries, long-live's, and shrieks from innumerable throats mixed with the sound of the wind, the waves, and the foghorns. Tograth was standing in the launch, tall and thin. As he approached, the hero's features came into focus. His face was clean-shaven and bluish where the hairs grew, his almost lipless mouth cut a large gash in his chinless face, so that he looked something like a shark. Above, his snub nose was punctured by two yawning nostrils. His forehead went straight up, very high and wide. His clothes were white, very tight, his shoes were also white with high heels. He wasn't wearing a hat. As soon as he set foot on the soil of Marseille, the enthusiasm was so great that when the docks were cleared three hundred people were found suffocated to death, stomped, and crushed. A few men grabbed the hero and lifted him up on their shoulders, while everyone sang and yelled as the women tossed flowers at him, all the way to the hotel where his rooms had been prepared, and where the managers, interpreters, and bellboys were waiting at the door.

▪

That same morning, Croniamantal, coming from Brunn, had arrived in Marseille to look for Tristouse, who had been there with Paponat since the night before. All three were in the crowd which was acclaiming Tograth in front of the hotel where he was staying.

"Marvelous uproar," said Tristouse. "You aren't a poet, Paponat, you learned things infinitely more valuable than poetry. You aren't a poet, Paponat, are you?"

"Well, my dear," replied Paponat, "I have versified to amuse myself, but I'm not a poet, I'm a very good businessman, and no one's better than I at managing a fortune."

"This evening you'll mail a letter to *The Voice* in Adelaide, you'll tell them all that and then you'll be safe."

"I'll do it for sure," said Paponat. "What a thing to be, a poet! It's all right for Croniamantal. . . ."

"I certainly hope," said Tristouse, "that they slaughter him in Brunn, where he thinks we are."

"But he's right over there," said Paponat quietly. "He's in the crowd. He's hidden, he hasn't seen us."

"I hope they massacre him right away," said Tristouse with a sigh. "I have the feeling it won't be long."

"Look," said Paponat, "here comes the hero."

▪

When the procession bringing Tograth had arrived in front of the hotel, they put the agronomist down on the ground. Tograth turned to the crowd and spoke:

"People of Marseille, to thank you I could use words larger than your famous sardine. I could make a long speech. But my words would never equal the magnificence of the reception you have reserved for me. I know that among you there are some afflicted with illness, whom I can help, thanks to science, not only mine but that which scientists have developed for thousands of years. Let the sick be brought to me, I want to heal them."

A man whose skull was as bald as a Myconian cried out:

"Tograth! Human divinity, oh most sapient and omnipotent, give me a luxurious growth of hair."

Tograth smiled and asked that this man be brought forth; then he touched the shining head, saying:

"Your sterile stone will be covered again with an abundant vegetation, but remember this happy event by hating the laurel forever."

A young girl had come forth the same time as the bald-headed man. She begged Tograth:

"Wonderful man, wonderful man, look at my mouth. My lover knocked some of my teeth out, give them back to me."

The scientist smiled and put his finger in her mouth, saying:

"You can bite now, you have perfect teeth. But, to thank me, show me what you have in your purse."

The girl laughed, opening her mouth where new teeth sparkled, then she opened her purse, excusing herself:

"It's sort of funny, in front of everyone. Here are my keys, here's the picture of my lover, a tintype; he's better than that."

But Tograth's eyes were shining; he had spotted, folded up, some rhymed Parisian songs written to Viennese tunes. He took these papers and examined them:

"These are just songs," he said, "you don't have any poems?"

"I have a very pretty one," said the girl, "the bellboy at the Hotel Victoria wrote it for me before he left for Switzerland. But I never showed it to Sossi."

And she handed Tograth a little pink piece of paper on which was written this lamentable acrostic:

M *y love, before I go and say farewell*
A *h! before our love, Maria, is derailed,*
R *uns wild and dies, while my heart still heaves,*
I *t would be nice to walk with you beneath the falling leaves*
A *nd then I'll leave you happy, I believe.*

"This is not only poetry," said Tograth, "it is, besides that, ridiculous."

He ripped up the paper and threw it in the gutter, as the girl's teeth chattered and she said, looking scared:

"Wonderful man, wonderful man, I didn't know it was bad."

At that moment, Croniamantal came up next to Tograth and harangued the crowd:

"Scum! Murderers!"

There was laughter. Someone shouted:

"Into the water with the fuckhead!"

And Tograth, looking at Croniamantal, said to him:

"My friend, may this crowd not offend you. As for myself, I love the mobs, although I stay in hotels they never frequent."

The poet let Tograth speak, then he turned back to the crowd:

"Scum, laugh at me, but your joys are numbered. They'll be taken from you one by one. And do you even know, you rabble, who your hero is?"

Tograth was smiling and the crowd had become attentive. The poet continued:

"Your hero, you rabble, is the Ennui that brings Evil."

A cry of astonishment was released from every breast. Some women made the sign of the cross. Tograth tried to speak, but Croniamantal seized him brusquely by the neck, threw him to the ground, and held him there with one foot on his chest. And he spoke:

"Yes it's Ennui and Evil, that monstrous enemy of man, the filthy, slimy Leviathan, the Behemoth polluted by the debauchery, rape, and blood of the marvelous poets. It is the vomit of the Antipodes, its miracles deceive the seers no more than the miracles of Simon the Magician deceived the Apostles. People of Marseille, why have you, whose ancestors came from the most purely lyric country, why have you joined the enemies of poetry, the savages of all nations? Do you know the strangest miracle of this German from Australia? It's having inspired such awe and for an instant having been more powerful than creation itself, more powerful than eternal poetry."

But Tograth, covered with dust and filled with rage, managed to stand up and demand:

"Who are you?"

And the crowd cried out:

"Who are you? Who are you?"

The poet turned to the east and said in an exalted voice:

"I am Croniamantal, the greatest living poet. I have often come face to face with God. I have withstood the divine blast, which my eyes tempered. I have lived eternity. But the time came for me to stand before you."

Tograth welcomed these last words with a burst of horrible laughter. The people up front, having seen Tograth laugh, laughed too, and the laughter, in bursts, in roulades, in trills, rolled over the entire populace, to Paponat and Tristouse Ballerinette. Croniamantal was faced with a sea of open mouths, and he was discountenanced. Among the laughter there were cries of:

"Into the water with him! . . . Burn Croniamantal! . . . Throw him to the dogs, the laurel-lover!"

A man in the first row who had a big club hit Croniamantal, whose painful expression redoubled the mob's laughter. A well-aimed rock hit the poet's nose, from which blood gushed out. A fishmonger elbowed her way through the crowd, up to Croniamantal, then said to him:

"Boo! You vulture! I recanize you, hey, you're that dirty cop that turned a poet, you pig liar!"

And she gave him a terrific wallop while spitting in his face. The man Tograth had cured of baldness came up saying:

"Look at this hair, you call that a false miracle, huh?"

And raising his cane, he thrust it so adroitly that it burst Croniamantal's right eye. He fell backwards. Some women fell upon him and beat him. Tristouse was prancing around with joy, as Paponat tried to calm her down. But with the point of her umbrella she went up and poked out Croniamantal's other eye, which saw her doing it. He cried out:

"I confess my love for Tristouse Ballerinette, the divine poetry that consoles my soul."

Then some men in the crowd cried out:

"Shut up, you bastard! Watch it ladies."

The ladies stepped quickly aside and a man wielding a butcherknife laid in his palm threw it so that it stuck right in Croniamantal's open mouth. Other men did the same. The knives stuck in his belly and chest, and pretty soon there was nothing left on the ground but a corpse spiked like a big sea urchin.

18. *Apotheosis*

Croniamantal dead, Paponat had taken Tristouse Ballerinette back to the hotel where she gave in to a typical nervous breakdown. They were in an old building and, by chance, Paponat discovered in a cupboard a bottle of Queen of Hungary Water which dated back to the seventeenth century. This remedy worked quickly. Tristouse came to her senses and without further delay went to the hospital to claim Croniamantal's body, which was given to her with no questions asked.

She gave him a decent funeral and on his grave placed a headstone, on which was engraved this epitaph:

TIPTOE

DO NOT DISTURB A GOOD LONG SLEEP

Then she returned to Paris with Paponat, who left her a few days later for a Champs-Elysées model.

Tristouse wasn't sorry about that for long. She went into mourning for Croniamantal and went to Montmartre, to the Bird of Benin, who began by courting her, and after he got what he wanted, they started talking about Croniamantal.

"I must do a statue for him," said the Bird of Benin. "Because I'm not only a painter, but a sculptor too."

"That's right," said Tristouse, "we must raise a statue for him."

"But where?" asked the Bird of Benin. "The government won't grant a place for it. It's a bad time for poets."

"That's what they say," replied Tristouse, "but perhaps it isn't true. What do you think of the Bois de Meudon, Mister Bird of Benin?"

"That's what I thought, but I didn't dare say so. It's the Bois de Meudon, then."

"A statue in what?" asked Tristouse. "Marble? Bronze?"

"No, that's too old-fashioned," replied the Bird of Benin. "I have to sculpt him a profound statue out of nothing, like poetry and glory."

"Bravo! Bravo!" said Tristouse clapping her hands, "a statue out of nothing, out of emptiness, it's magnificent—when will you do it?"

"Tomorrow, if you like. Let's go have dinner, spend the night together, and early tomorrow morning we'll go to the Bois de Meudon where I'll sculpt that profound statue."

▪

No sooner said than done. They had dinner with the elite of Montmartre, came back and went to bed around midnight, and at nine o'clock the next morning, equipped with a pick, a spade, a scoop, and the rough sketches, they headed toward the pretty Bois de Meudon, where they met, in the company of his darling, the Prince of Poets, very happy with the pleasant days he had spent at the Conciergerie.

In the clearing, the Bird of Benin went to work. In a few hours, he hollowed out a hole about a half yard wide and two yards deep.

After that they had a picnic lunch.

The Bird of Benin devoted the afternoon to sculpting the interior of the monument to resemble Croniamantal.

The next day the sculptor came back with some workers who prepared the pit with a wall of reinforced concrete about eight centimeters thick, except at the bottom, where it was thirty-eight. This way the void was shaped like Croniamantal, the hole was filled with his phantom.

▪

Two days later the Bird of Benin, Tristouse, the Prince of Poets, and his darling returned to the monument, which was filled in with the dirt that had been taken out of it, and there, with night fallen, a fine poet's laurel was planted, as Tristouse Ballerinette danced, singing:

All do not love you you lie
Palantila mila milie
When he was lover of the queen
He was king since she was queen
It's true it's true

That I love you
At the bottom of the pit oh might
It be him
Gather sweet marjoram
At night

THE MOON KING

TO RENÉ BERTIER

1.

On February 23, 1912 I was hiking across that part of the Tyrol which begins almost at the edge of Munich. It was freezing cold. The sun had been shining all day. I had left far behind me a region where fabulous castles were reflected in pink lakes at dusk. Night had fallen, the full moon was shining, a floating block in the firmament where cold stars were glittering. It could have been five o'clock. I was hurrying because I wanted to be on time for dinner at the Grand Hotel in Werp, a town well known by mountain climbers and which, according to the map I had in my pocket, shouldn't have been more than a few miles away. The path had become bad. I came to a crossroad where four paths ended. I was going to consult my map when I discovered that I'd lost it on the way. Then again, the spot I was in corresponded to no point on the itinerary I clearly remembered: I was lost. There wasn't much time. And the idea of sleeping on the ground didn't appeal to me. I took the path that seemed headed toward Werp. After walking half an hour I stopped where the path ended at the foot of a stone cliff about fifty yards high, behind which rose a chaotic mass of mountains white with snow. Around me big pines swayed their somber, drooping shapes—the wind had come up, tops crashing together, their lugubrious sound adding to the horror of the wilderness chance had led me into. I realized that it would be impossible to reach Werp before dawn, so I began looking for some grotto, some crag to shelter me from the wind until dawn. As I was carefully examining the cliff, which went straight up in front of me, I thought I saw an opening. I went over. I made out a very spacious cavern and I ventured inside. Outside, the wind was howling and the soughing of the pines had something poignant about it, as if thousands of travelers were crying out in despair. After a few minutes, having gotten used to the cavern, I perceived a distant sound of music. I first thought I was wrong, but soon there was no doubt about it: sonorous, harmonious waves were rolling up to my ears from the bowels of the mountain. Astonishment and terror! I wanted out of there. But then curiosity got the better of me, and, feeling my way along the wall, I proceeded to explore this den of sorcery. As I went along like this for more than a quarter of an hour, the harmonies of the underground orchestra became more distinct; then the wall made an abrupt turn. Making the turn, I noticed, at a distance I couldn't judge, a small amount of light, filtering, it seemed, around a window shutter. I picked up my pace and was soon standing in front of a door.

The music had stopped. I could hear a murmur of distant voices. Telling myself that, after all, subterranean music lovers shouldn't be dangerous, and, again, since I couldn't bring myself to admit—despite the evidence—that my adventure had a supernatural origin, I knocked twice on the door. But no one came. Finally, finding a latch with my hand and releasing it and meeting no resistance, I entered a vast, dim hall, walls faced with colored marble and shells in the half-light, as water trickled into basins swimming with multicolored fish.

2.

It was only after looking around for a long time that I saw a door at the end of this grotto. I peeked into the next room, which was very large and had a very high ceiling. It was a sort of dining hall, furnished, in the middle, with a round table large enough to seat more than a hundred guests. At the moment there were about fifty there, young people from fifteen to twenty-five years old, all chattering away.

From the door I was at, and where I could not be seen, I noticed that the table had no legs. It was suspended from the ceiling by four metal hooks attached to pulleys, over which ran metal cables. From these pulleys the cables went off in different directions along the ceiling, and, passing through rings attached to the cornices, came down the walls, so that the table could be lowered, raised, and held in place. There was a similar arrangement for the seats in that strange dining room. They all looked like swings. Electric lights shone forth in different colored bulbs. I noticed that all the colors of the prism were there and that, hanging down on their wires, these bulbs were disposed at random over the entire room at different heights. There were even some coming out of the baseboards. All these multicolored lights were so well distributed that the room appeared to be bathed in sunlight.

I saw no servants, but in a moment, after the guests had enough of the dishes that had been served to them, the valets came in from the far doors to take away the first setting, while other servants came in pushing a cart, on which, lashed down on a bed of dry wood, lay a live ox. When the cart, whose bottom could give off enough electric heat to cook a roast, was near the table, it was lit, forming an instantaneous and aromatic brazier over which the live ox was turned. At this moment four carvers came forward with that tired, satisfied look of my friend René Bertier, when, before leaving the domain of science for that of poetry, or vice versa, he uses a nail file to open his daily can of pineapple. The guests, who were chattering pleasantly, immediately interrupted their conversations to pick their favorite cut, the way business journalists do after a new colonial conquest. The live ox was sliced up accordingly, but so skillful was the butcher that each piece was detached and roasted without touching any of the essential organs. Soon only the skin and bones were left. They were taken away, like a taxpayer devoured by the tax collectors.

Then twenty fowlers came in, bird calls between their lips, each man carrying two cages full of live, plucked ducks, which were throttled in front of each guest. The wine waiters, appearing spontaneously, filled the glasses with Hungarian wine, and twenty trumpeters came in through four doors at the same time and began blowing on their instruments, from which hung flags and ribbons.

▪

This meal of living foods seemed so odd to me that I began to wonder about my own fate at the hands of these bloodthirsty people, but then they got up from the table, and while some lit cigarettes, some cigars, the valets cleared the table, which, along with the chairs, was shot up to the ceiling. The room was now empty of furniture. The trumpeters were replaced by four blind violinists playing popular tunes, which inspired these young people to dance. But this exercise lasted for no more than fifteen minutes, after which they went out and into another room.

▪

The door was left open, so I tiptoed over. In the other room they were chatting away, while around them strange furniture seemed to dance about in the oddest way, and without music. This furniture rose little by little, like a fashionable poet giving a reading, and waddled along, rising and growing jerkily. Soon it began to look like comfortable furniture, leather armchairs and divans. One table looked like a mushroom. It too was covered with leather.

As soon as the furniture had stopped gasping and began to look like real furniture, the strangers sat down and continued to smoke. Four of them moved in around the table and got up a game of bridge, which immediately provoked the most disagreeable discussion, to the extent that one of them, his face red with anger, put his lit cigar down on the table while discussing an opponent's hand, and the table suddenly exploded, like a German dirigible, somewhat disturbing the card game and the company. A Negro immediately ran over to take out the pneumatic table which had exploded at the touch of the cigar and was lying on the ground like a dead elephant. He offered to bring another one of those leather-covered rubber tables, a new sort of furniture that could be inflated and deflated at will and therefore very convenient, even when traveling. But the gentlemen said they didn't feel like playing anymore. So the Negro deflated the furniture, which collapsed like a Russian servant hissing before his master. Then everyone left the unfurnished smoking room and the Negro turned out the lights.

3.

Finding myself abruptly in darkness, I went over to the wall and proceeded in the direction of the dying voices. Feeling my way, I came to a stairway, at the bottom of which was a door opening onto a narrow corridor cut through the rock, on whose surface I saw, either chiseled or written in pencil or charcoal, the most extraordinary obscene graffiti. I quote those I remember, avoiding the crudity of certain words used.

A monstrous double phallus bloomed from the initial M in the following inscription:

MICHÆLANGELO REALLY TURNED ON
HANS VON JAGOW

This was written in pencil.

Further along, an arrow surrounded by a snake was piercing a heart, from which there was an unfurled banderole with this motto:

TO CLEOPATRA FOR LIFE

A scholar had used gothic characters to formulate an astounding wish referring to Hrotswitha, the dramatist:

I'D LOVE TO MAKE LOVE
WITH
THE ABBESS OF GANDERSHEIM

The history of France had inspired an anonymous admirer of the eighteenth century to make the most delirious exclamation:

I MUST HAVE
MADAME DE POMPADOUR

These inscriptions were cut into the wall with a metallic point.

Here is one, in chalk, accompanied by three winged kteis in different sizes:

IN ONE NIGHT I HAD THE SAME
PRETTY TYROLEAN OF THE 17TH CENTURY
WHEN SHE WAS 16, 21, AND 23
I COULD HAVE HAD HER
WHEN SHE WAS 70 BUT
I GAVE NICHOLAS A CHANCE

Anglomania was at its height in this categorical declaration in blue pencil:

THE NAMELESS ENGLISH GIRL
IN CROMWELL'S TIME
GOBBLES EVERYTHING

Signed WILLY HORN

One inscription written in big charcoal letters and nearly erased in spots seemed to me a burst of sarcastic laughter, almost inappropriate in this unimaginable graphic graveyard:

LAST NIGHT I HAD THE COUNTESS TERNISKA
AT THE AGE OF 17 SHE WHO
WAS A GOOD 45

H. VON M.

And finally, I don't think I was too bold, considering the preceeding graffiti, and despite the unlikelihood of its supposition, to attribute this candid and passionate avowal to the minion of King Henry III:

I LOVE QUELUS MADLY

These equivocal and enigmatic inscriptions filled me with stupefaction. Pierced hearts, flaming hearts, double hearts, still other emblems: "pussies," winged or not, bald or furry; proud or humble phalluses, with big paws or taking flight, alone or accompanied by their "mates." All these decorated the walls with an indecent and whimsical heraldry.

I continued resolutely down the corridor until, through a door, half of which was a heavy tapestry, I saw what was happening in a room whose floor was padded and covered with rugs, cushions, and platters loaded with refreshments. On the lower part of the walls were a few basins with faucets shaped like prows—these could be used as bidets or washbasins. The squad of young people I had been following about had ended up lying down in this room. Also on the padded floor were some wooden boxes. Each of these gentlemen had one nearby. Others weren't being used, and one of them, near the door, was within my reach.

They were completely absorbed looking through some albums, of which there were a great many. From a distance it seemed to me that they were collections of nude photographs: professional artists' models, men, women, and children.

When the expected effect of these nudes was produced, these young people struck the most unbecoming postures imaginable. They fully displayed their vigor and, opening the boxes, they started the machines, which began to turn slowly, something like phonograph cylinders. They buckled on a sort of belt which was connected to the machine, and it seemed to me that they all must have looked like Ixion when he caressed the Phantom of Clouds, the invisible Hera. The hands of these young men strayed in front of them as if over supple, beloved bodies, and they gave the air amorous kisses. Soon they became more lascivious and irrepressible and wedded themselves to the emptiness. I was taken aback, as if I had witnessed the disturbing games of a college of priapic maniacs. Sounds escaped from their lips, words of love, voluptuous gasps, very ancient names, among which I recognized those of the very wise Heloise, of Lola Montez, of an octoroon from I don't know which eighteenth-century Louisiana plantation; someone spoke of a "page, my handsome page."

This anachronistic orgy suddenly reminded me of the inscriptions in the corridor. I listened more attentively to the lascivious language and witnessed the performance of every desire of these libertines, who were finding sensuality in the arms of death.

"The boxes," I told myself, "are cemeteries where these necrophiles dig up amorous corpses."

This idea carried me away. I found myself in sympathy with these debauchees and, reaching out, I seized the box near the door without anyone noticing. I opened it and started it up, as I had seen the others do, girded my loins, and immediately there materialized before my ravished eyes a naked body which was smiling up at me voluptuously.

▪

Not being mechanically minded, it would be difficult for me to hold forth on the nature of the machine or the theories which had underlain its construction. Nevertheless, since its appearance was in no way supernatural, I tried to imagine how it worked.

The purpose of this machine was, on the one hand, to abstract from time a certain portion of space and to fix it at a certain moment and for a few minutes only, because the machine wasn't very powerful; and on the other hand to make visible and tangible to whoever wore the belt that portion of time brought back to life.

This is how I was able to look at, feel, and, in a word, work at (not without difficulty) the body within my grasp, while this body had no notion of my presence, having itself no current reality.

These machines must have been set up at great expense, because patience alone, on the part of the inventor, could have brought him to meet these voluptuous characters at the height of their passion, and much probing must have been necessary, and many cylinders must have met with only unimportant people doing anything but making love.

I would guess that an elaborate study of history, especially chronology, must have been indispensable to the builders. They aimed their machine at the spot where they knew that at a certain date a certain woman had lain down, and, setting the machine in motion, had it reach the precise moment when they could encounter the subject in the proper attitude.

Machines more powerful and built for an end more in keeping with current morals could serve to reconstruct historic scenes. No doubt the use of phonetic equipment would permit the inventor, if he wished to make public his secret, instead of having it serve only as an amusement for a few underground debauchees, would permit, I say, the complete picture of a fragmented past, with explorers of time past, just as there still are—but not for long—explorers of unknown lands. One of these explorers would try, roll by roll, to reconstruct the life of Napoleon. Newspapers would publish articles such as: "Mr. X . . . , the time explorer, has just, through a lucky accident, discovered the poet Villon, of whose life so little is known still, and cylinder by cylinder, he is following him step by step."

▪

But let us not anticipate. All this is still in the realm of utopia, whereas the body I held in my arms seemed so pleasurable to me that I made liberal use of it without its suspecting a thing.

It was a dark and voluptuous woman with white skin and so many delicate dark blue veins that she appeared to be blue, that wonderful navy blue out of which the foam condensed into what was the divine body of Aphrodite. And with her arms out in front of her, breast-high, she seemed to be pushing something back—I imagined it to be the white and flexible body of the swan which will never sing and that she was Leda, mother of the Dioscuri. Soon she disappeared when the machine stopped and then I tiptoed away, overwhelmed by my good fortune.

4.

Back in the corridor, the silly graffiti and the famous names filled me with disgust, but so proud was I of being henceforth linked to the horrible house of the Tyndarides that I was unable to refrain from writing in pencil:

I HAVE CUCKOLDED THE SWAN

Then, upset, unable to bear the unfamiliar atmosphere of that subterranean but certainly not supernatural house, I began looking for a way out without being seen. But I lost my way, because instead of going back through the previous rooms, I soon found myself, shaking all over, in a large hall where, on a platform with three steps, there was a seat with broken legs, a sort of dislocated throne, behind which hung a tapestry showing a coat of arms, silver and blue. On the wall with the door I had come through there were paintings depicting life in colored zones and bright lights.

An organ completely dominated the far wall, and side by side, like knights in armor, the polished pipes stood watch. On the organ lay a finely bound musical score, bearing on its cover:

ORIGINAL SCORE FOR 'DAS RHINEGOLD'

The room was paved with ophite, black marble, and copper. There were also some transparent glass bricks, through which light filtered, red or violet. This light wasn't enough for the room: artificial light poured through large fake windows like real sunlight. I saw pools of blood at certain spots on the floor, and in a corner a heap of strange crowns made of gilded copper and glass.

▪

It was here that the most exciting event of my trip took place. I wanted out of there but didn't dare double back, so I took a chance and, without making the slightest sound, opened a little door near the organ. It was about eight o'clock in the evening. I glanced into a larger hall which was lit no worse than the one I was in and which was completely scented with essence of roses.

There I saw a man with a young face (though he was about sixty-five years old), dressed like a high French aristocrat from the reign of Louis XVI. His hair, braided like Panurge's, was heavy with powder and pomade. As I noticed later, scenes from *Richard the Lion-Hearted* were embroidered on his vest, whose buttons, two inches wide, contained portraits of the twelve Caesars under glass.

Around the room copper pavilions emerged from the walls.

This strange character, whose anachronistic look formed such a contrast to the metallic modernity of that room, was sitting at a keyboard, one of whose keys he pressed with a weary finger. It remained depressed, while out of one pavilion came a strange and continuous sound which I was unable to identify at first.

For a moment the stranger listened carefully to these sounds. Suddenly he arose and, with a gesture at once effeminate and theatrical, the right hand extended, the left on his heart, he cried, as the procession of oral vistas came forward:

"Hermit kingdom! O land of Calm Morning! The first blush of dawn on your territory and already the prayers are rising from your monasteries and this precise machine is bringing me the sound. I hear the rustlings of oil-paper vests, the kind commoners wear, and I hear the storm of alms raining down on the scuffling paupers. I hear you too, bronze clock of Seoul. In your voice I hear a child crying. I also hear a procession following its fine lord, the magnificent Yang Ban in his saddle. If some day I, the Moon King, wear once again the pale purple which is properly mine alone, I shall visit your setting and enjoy your climate, which is said to be delicious."

And while these words were rolling forth from the man I immediately recognized to be King Ludwig II of Bavaria, I realized that the common belief held in Bavaria, that their insane, unfortunate king did not perish in the murky waters of the Starnbergersee, was correct. But the distant sounds coming from the sad kingdom of the monasteries claimed my attention so that I had to let myself fall under the spell coming over me from the land of white clothing. And, listening carefully to the murmuring dawn, I thought I heard washerwomen forever beating the linens and virginal clothes and the incessant thwacks of the sticks replacing the steam iron, as if it were the white dawn itself being washed and ironed.

Then this majestic victim of a fake Starnbergersee drowning pressed another key, and, from what the king said I understood that the sounds which were coming to us evoked the happy ambiance of Japan precisely at dawn.

The flawless microphones of the king's device were set so as to bring in to this underground the most distant sounds of terrestrial life. Each key activated a microphone set for such-and-such a distance. Now we were hearing a Japanese countryside. The wind soughed in the trees—a village was probably there, because I heard servants' laughter, a carpenter's plane, and the spray of an icy waterfall.

Then, another key pressed down, we were taken straight into morning, the king greeting the socialist labor of New Zealand, and I heard geysers spewing hot water.

Then this wonderful morning continued in sweet Tahiti. Here we are at the market in Papeete, with the lascivious wahinees of New Cytheria wandering through it—you could hear their lovely guttural language, very much like ancient Greek. You could also hear the Chinese selling tea, coffee, butter, and cakes. The sound of accordions and Jew's harps. . . .

Now we're in America, the plains are immense, no doubt a town has sprung up here around the train station where the Pullman is pulling out again, and along with the king I hear its whistle.

Terrible noises of the street, streetcars, factories—we seem to be in Chicago and it is noon.

Now New York, the vessels singing on the Hudson.

Violent prayers before a Christ in Mexico.

It is four o'clock. A carnivalesque cavalcade in Rio de Janeiro goes by. Rubber balls, perfectly aimed, splatter against the faces and spread a perfume, the way the Moorish *alcancias* did long ago, plick, plock, laughter, ah! ah!

It is six o'clock in Saint Pierre, Martinique. People wearing masks and singing are on their way to the balls decorated with huge red cana flowers. You hear them singing:

Who don' know,
Hon, halfbreed Belo,
Who don' know,
Halfbreed Robelo.

Seven o'clock, Paris. I recognized the shrill voice of Mr. Ernst L. J..n.ss., because the microphone happened to lead up to a cafe on the "grands boulevards."

The angelus rings at the Munster in Bonn and a boat with a double chorus singing passes along the Rhine on its way to Coblenz.

Then Italy near Naples. The coachmen were playing scissors-paper-rock in the starry night.

Then came Tripoli where, around a bivouac campfire, M.r.n.tt. was practicing his "pidgin," while troops from the House of Savoy were surrounding him, like soldiers, ready to defend him in the unlikely event of an attack, and firing a few onomatopoeic shots, while across the camp, from post to post, the bugles were answering one another.

A minute later, ten o'clock! Are these beggars, whining and moaning so? The king listens to them and mutters,

"It's the voice of Ispahan coming in, born of a night black as the blood of poppies."

And while he daydreams I imagine the scent of jasmines.

Midnight! A poor shepherd cries out in an icy waste: it is nocturnal Asia, from which evil rolls out over the world.

Elephants roar. One o'clock in the morning! India!

Then Tibet. The sacerdotal clocks chiming.

Three o'clock: the sounds of thousands of boats softly bumping each other on the shores of the river in Saigon.

Doom doom boom, doom doom boom, Peking, gongs and tambourines keeping time to a dance, and innumerable dogs yapping and barking into the gloomy sound of the dancing. A rooster crows to announce the livid dawn that is already fleeing over white Korea.

The king's fingers ran over the keys at random, simultaneously raising all the sounds of this world which we, standing still, had just toured aurally.

While I stood there amazed, the king suddenly looked up. At first he didn't seem at all surprised by my presence.

"Bring me," he said to me, "the original score for *Das Rhinegold*—I'd like to run over it after listening to the symphony of the world, and before hearing the walking orchestra of Mr. Oswald von Hartfield.... Wait a minute, criminal face, where is your mask? I don't want anyone in my presence without a mask."

And, his own face suddenly vicious, the king came toward me, his fists clenched. He was built like Hercules. He shook me hard, hit and kicked me, and spit in my face, screaming,

"Off with his testicles! Frankenstein, Eulenburg, Jacob Ernst, Durkheim, off with his testicles!"

I didn't wait for any of these gentlemen to appear. But realizing that the king was more upset by my lack of a mask than by my simple presence, I told myself that if I could find my way back out of there, no one would come after me, since the king had mistaken me for one of his household: servants, subalterns, pages, lords, and boatmen.

And when I ran out I heard him yelling,

"The score for *Das Rhinegold*, a mask for your ugly mug or off with your testicles!"

5.

So once again I was wandering around in that sumptuous underground inhabited by this old drowned man who had been a mad king. For at least two hours I advanced cautiously in the dark, opening doors, feeling my way along the walls, finding no exit.

At first I heard voices in the distance, then everything fell silent.

Finally I found myself once again in the grotto which served as a vestibule to the unbelievable place.

Outside, someone blew a fanfare, then stopped. All I had to do was open the door through which I had entered the hypogeum and walk out into the pines.

But the forest was illuminated. The thousand lights which had been born there ran along, rose, fell, went off, came back, came together, bunched up, came fluttering down, went out, came on, shrank, expanded, changed colors, brought their tints together, modified these colors, flew into geometric shapes, flew apart glimmering, flaming, shooting sparks, fizzling, solidified so to speak into incandescent geometric forms, into letters of the alphabet, numbers, into animated shapes of men and animals, into high burning columns, into rolling lakes of flaming waves, into pale phosphorescences, into spurting rockets, in girandoles, in light with no visible source, in beams, in zigzags.

From time to time I could see a whole crowd of people in the distance. Hiding behind trees and working my way toward them, I came close enough to make them out. They all wore masks, except the old king, who was barefaced. He was dressed half masculine, half feminine; that is, over his eighteenth-century clothing he wore a hoop gown, but open in front and set off by a belt, the kind firemen wear.

At this moment the music started again. Some of the musicians were far away, others were quite close. Their fanfares faded away and returned, blaring near and far. It was as if a hundred orchestras were receding, seeking each other, regrouping, running after one another, going off or coming back close together, fast or slow. There were unknown strident notes, sonorities of fantastic force, and sensationally novel timbres. The music came from very high up, as if from the sky. It came from underground and we were drowned, so to speak, in an ocean of magic sound.

All of a sudden these people put on belts like the one the king was wearing. As some had turned toward me, I could see that on the front the belt was decorated with an instrument rather like an alarm clock.

"*That* is color," the king said, "and this is the greatest of all the arts—it is richer than painting. . . . And this shifting music, is it not really alive? Now, my friends, let us go for a stroll."

▪

The Moon King gracefully flew up and perched in a tree, where he continued speaking. But I couldn't make out what he was saying; it seemed to me he was chirping at the moon glimmering through the branches. Then he took off again. Everyone else took off with him and they disappeared into the air like a flock of migratory birds.

I succeeded in making Werp by morning, and, for a long time, I didn't feel the need to tell anyone about my experiences.

GIOVANNI MORONI

TO SERGE JASTREBZOFF AND EDOUARD FÉRAT

There are now, as in all countries, moreover, so many foreigners in France that it is not without interest to study the sensibilities of those among them who, born elsewhere, came however at an age young enough to be shaped by high French civilization. They bring to their adopted country their childhood impressions, the strongest of all, and enrich the spiritual patrimony of their new nation the way chocolate and coffee, for example, extended the domain of taste.

Not long ago I knew a fellow named Giovanni Moroni, a person of no great culture. He was employed in a bank. Italian by birth, he had come to France at an early age to live with one of his uncles, a grocer in Montmartre. Giovanni Moroni was a man about thirty, husky, quick to laugh, indecisive. He had forgotten Italian. His conversation hardly ever exceeded everyday banalities. However, one day I heard him talking about his early years, and this wanderer's story seemed to me compelling and flavorful enough to transcribe.

▪

My mother's name was Attilia. My father, Beppo Moroni, made wooden toys, delivered for a few pennies to the big dealers who sold them at much higher prices. He complained about this often. I had all kinds of toys: horses, Punches, swords, bowling pins, puppets, soldiers, wagons. All were wooden, and often I made so much noise and such a mess that my mother threw up her hands, crying:

"Holy Mother! What a good-for-nothing. Ah Giovannino, you've been like this ever since you were baptized. While the priest sprinkled water on your face, you were wetting your diaper."

And good Attila bestowed upon me a few hard knocks which I tried to fend off while bawling and sobbing hopelessly.

That period of my childhood in Rome left me some very precise memories.

The most distant go back to the age of three.

I see myself looking at a wood fire in the fireplace and watching a pine cone catch fire and pop out of its alveoles the almonds that were as hard as bone and even looked like bone.

I remember the Feast of the Epiphany. I was happy to have new toys, which I believed to have been brought by Befana, that sort of ugly old fairy, like Morgana, but nice to children and kindhearted. These feast days for the Three Kings, when I ate so many candied orange peels, so many anise drops, have left me with a delicious aftertaste!

During the day, despite the cold, I stayed with my father in the booth he kept in the Piazza Navona where he had a concession, for that week, to peddle his toys. Beppo let me run from one booth to another, and, in the evening, Attilia, bringing her husband's dinner and coming to fetch me for bed, had to look for me quite a while, lamenting that maybe some gypsies had carried me away.

I also remember the torture of the cockroaches, which came back every month. My mother somehow got them all together, in an old barrel, and I was allowed to witness their passing. She dumped boiling water on the unfortunate bugs, whose final agitation, running, and chaotic jumping enchanted me.

▪

Outside of Befana time, my mother took me out with her for walks, while her husband was working at home.

She was a pretty brunette, still young. The sergeants twirled their moustaches when they went past. I loved her very much, especially because she had very heavy big gold rings for earrings. It was by this detail that I judged her superior to my father, who had on his ears only some little circles, thin as thread.

When we went out we went to the churches, to the Pincio, to the Corso, to watch the beautiful carriages going by. In winter, before going home, my mother bought me hot chestnuts, and, in the summer, a slice of watermelon, cold as lightly sweetened ice cream.

Often we came home late, and then there were arguments which sometimes were horrible. My mother was thrown on the floor, dragged about by the hair. I can clearly see my father trampling on my mother's breast, because during the fight the blouse tore or opened and her breasts stood out, stigmatized by the hobnail boots.

Despite this unpleasantness, rather rare, besides, my parents got along well.

▪

I was five years old when I had my first real scare.

One day my mother got all dressed up and put my prettiest frock on me. Then we went out. My mother bought a bouquet of violets. We came to a seedy neighborhood, an old house. We climbed a stairway whose steps of narrow and crooked stone were worn slick. An old woman showed us into a room furnished with a few new chairs. Then a man came in. He was thin, rather badly dressed. His eyes burned strangely and his eyelids had no lashes and were turned back. You could see the repulsive bright red skin around the eyes. Frightened, I grabbed my mother's skirts, but she threw herself on her knees before the man, who threatened and gave orders. I fainted and came to only in the street. My mother said to me:

"You are so stupid! What were you afraid of?"

And I cried:

"I'll tell daddy, I'll tell daddy."

She consoled me and calmed me down by buying me a little tamarind paste, which I liked very much.

▪

One other time, my mother had a toothache.

That evening, as she suffered, her husband teased her and joked, saying:

"It's the pain of love."

That night I was put to bed earlier than usual. The next day the pain persisted. My mother had to go to the Capuchins.

The doorman showed us into a parlor decorated with a crucifix, pious pictures, olive branches, and palms that had been blessed.

Around the table some brothers were arranging baskets of tiny salads, with lettuce, purslane, radish leaves, bloodwort, and nasturtiums, which these monks usually sold in town. An old Capuchin came in and blessed me, while my mother kissed his hands and made the sign of the cross. My mother sat down, the Capuchin wrapped a napkin around some forceps, set himself behind the patient, and inserted the instrument in her mouth. The operating surgeon made an effort and a face. My mother gave out a howl and started to run, with me hanging on her skirts. At the monastery door she remembered having forgotten to take the extracted tooth. She went back to the parlor, and, after some words of thanks, asked for it back. The monk blessed us while saying that the teeth he pulled were the only fee he asked. Since then I've thought that these teeth probably became holy relics, and rightly so.

▪

My mother was given to superstition. I admit that I don't look down on it either. Causes are linked. Finding a four-leaf clover indicates a future happiness, perhaps. There's nothing incredible in that. In Strasbourg, storks arrive just before spring and announce it, and no one would want to doubt it.

One time, in summer, my mother had been given the address of a monk who told fortunes cheaply. He lived alone in a deserted monastery and showed us into a library whose very floor was heaped with books. There were also spheres, musical and astronomical instruments. The monk was a handsome boy who wore a crown of thick, dark hair. His robe was stained with wine and grease and dirtied with stiff, dry little spots. He gestured to a chair for my mother, who sat down and put me on her knee. He took his place in an armchair on the other side of a table littered with one half-empty bottle and another still full, through the neck of which shone, like a topaz, the oil serving as cork. Also on the table were an escritoire, a dirty glass, and a filthy deck of cards. The operation lasted half an hour, taking all my mother's attention, while I watched only the fortune teller, whose robe had opened and showed him bare beneath. He had the audacity, when the cards were used up, to stand up that way, bestially shameless, and to refuse the fifty centimes my mother offered him while pretending she didn't notice.

It seems that this monk's sorcery was valuable for my mother, since she went back to him. But he must have scared her, because she always took me along to protect her.

One time the monk handed her a sachet containing a small piece of gold, another with silver, a small *osso di morto*, and a magnet. He told my mother not to forget to feed the magnet every week a little crumb of bread soaked in wine and to be sure to remove the magnet's dejecta.

Another time, the monk had prepared a wooden triangle on which little candles had been stuck. He advised my mother, who, that evening, when my father was out for some air, lit the candles and carried the triangle to the latrines while uttering strange words that scared me. When she threw it into the trench, great clouds of smoke issued forth and we ran off, each as frightened as the other.

The last time we went to the monk's he gave my mother a piece of mirror, saying:

"This is a piece of the mirror in which Torlonia, the richest man in Italy, looked at himself. And know that while you look into it you become like the person who owns it. So, if I had given you a prostitute's mirror, you would become like her, shameless."

His eyes were shining and looking ardently at my mother, who looked away as she took the mirror.

▪

. . . Because I haven't seen Rome again since my childhood, I have only a few vague and fragmented memories of it. I'm sorry I can't place the following adventure in the exact frame of the Roman Carnival. But I was only a child, and, carried in my father's arms, saw only the wagons with *confettaci*, boxes of sweetmeats, and flowers falling from them.

One evening during Carnival, my parents, four friends, and I were at table with the dish for that occasion: a pie-plate of macaroni with gravy mixed with chicken liver, which was to be followed by a sweet pie-plate of macaroni with sugar and cinnamon.

Suddenly, someone beat on the door and drunken voices demanded that we open it.

My father said, "It's some guys celebrating Carnival, come to play some pranks, drink at our expense, rouse our curiosity, and then go off and do the same thing elsewhere. It's Carnival, you have to have a good time."

And he went to open the door: a troop of masks invaded the apartment. One of them was carried by four of his companions. There was one harlequin, a Pagliacci, a French cook, two Punches, etc. The one being carried was wearing a half-red, half-black costume, his mask bearded. I was afraid and started crying, while the masks sang and my mother went to look for three bottles of wine. For there was none on the table, because you drink only water with the macaroni.

When the wine was there, one of the carriers cried:

"Hey, drunk! Hey, sleepy! Hey, dead drunk! Here's some wine. Stand on your own."

Another carrier added:

"Ah, I've had enough, let's put him on the table. Our friend can't drink a bottle without falling down dead drunk. . . ."

My mother had quickly cleared the table. They laid the sleeping mask on it. Then they all drank boisterously.

"To your health!" said one of them to the sleeper, "and from now on hold your wine better!"

Another one threw a full glass on him, sneering:

"That'll be good for you, my boy."

Then the one who had spoken first went on in a peremptory tone:

"Now, are you coming, yes or no? I know very well that you are no more asleep than I am. You're pretending. Come on or we'll leave without you. I don't feel like breaking my back carrying you. Come on! The joke's gone too far."

But the man did not budge. So one of the masks said, as his companions moved toward the door:

"We don't want to be dragged down by a lazy slob. It's a feast day, phooey on sleepers. He's fine on the table. He won't take long to wake up and find his own way back."

"We are not living in the time of the Duke de Borso!" cried my father. "You jokers take your drunken friend with you!"

And he ran after the masks who were already going downstairs singing:

Our banner has three parts:
The green for hope,
The white pure as our hearts,
The red . . .

But soon my father came back, saying:

"They can't hear anything. They're soused. Come on, Attilia, bring us some water. We'll wake him up all right."

But already one of my father's friends was tearing off the sleeper's mask. Then a cry of horror escaped from every breast. The face of a dark, handsome man had appeared, his eye sockets splattered with blood. My father rushed over and opened the man's costume. He bore two wounds near the heart. The murder must have been recent, because the blood was still flowing and had soaked through the costume. But until then it had been taken for stains from wine or some other drink.

A paper had been placed on the murdered man's chest. My father took the note and read it aloud:

Bice loved you for your blue eyes. I have emptied them like mussel shells.

My mother opened the window and called for the guard. The police came soon with the neighbors. But I was carried out and I learned nothing more about the affair.

▪

At that time I was seven years old. My father tried to teach me to spell. But I didn't relish his lessons and preferred to play Odds and Evens by myself, which is hard, but possible.

When I wasn't playing Odds and Evens, I would say Mass. A chair became the altar, which I decked out with little candelabra, ciboria, and lead monstrances which Befana had brought me. Sometimes I rode a stick which had a horse's head on the end. Finally, when I had tired of all these games, I took refuge in a corner with Maldino. This character held a great place in my life. He was a puppet painted green, yellow, blue, and red. I loved him more than any of my other toys, because I had seen him being carved by my foster father.

His strange birth, at which I had presided, and his coloring combined to make him for me a sort of genius which I liked to believe was tutelary. I don't know why I named him Maldino. I invented names for everything that struck me. One time I saw a fish on the kitchen table. I thought about it a long time, then named it Binoulor.

One day I was chatting with Maldino, because I imagined that the puppet answered me, when someone rang. It was St. Joseph's Day. My father had gone out. It was his name day, and, on this one, he dedicated it to drinking. My mother opened the door and led in a thin, graying gentleman. He asked to speak to my father.

"Beppo is out," said my mother, "but I'm his wife."

The gentleman handed her an envelope, saying:

"In that case, you can read the letter."

But Attilia burst out laughing, lowered her eyes, and replied, blushing:

"I don't know how to read."

At that moment my father came in, lightly salted. When he had read the visitor's letter he looked at his wife and whispered in her ear. She burst into tears.

My father's heart was softened by the libations, and he started crying with my mother, and, seeing their tears, I started crying harder than he. Only the stranger seemed cold, but he respected our despair.

When I had cried myself out, I went to sleep and woke up in a moving train. The only person I saw in the compartment was my father. Fortunately I felt my genius in my arms, my Maldino. My father was looking out the door. I did the same. Landscapes slid past beneath my gaze, interrupted at every moment by telegraph poles. The staves formed by the telegraph lines went down, then suddenly rose up, to my astonishment. The train made a solid iron music which rocked me: bururboom boom boom, bururboom boom boom. I fell asleep again and woke up when the train stopped. I rubbed my eyes. My father said to me softly:

"Giovannino, look."

I looked and saw behind the station a leaning tower.

It was Pisa. I was amazed and raised Maldino so he could see that tower about to fall over. When the train was moving again, I took my father's hand and asked him:

"Where's mommy?"

"She's at home," my father said. "You'll write to her when you know how to write, and you'll come back when you're big."

"But tonight, I won't see her?"

"No," my father answered sadly, "you won't see her tonight."

I started crying and hitting him, shouting:

"Dirty liar!"

But he soothed me, saying:

"Giovannino, be good. Tonight we'll be in Turin and I'll take you to see Giandouia, who looks like your favorite puppet, only bigger."

I looked at Maldino tenderly, and I consoled myself with the idea of going to see a larger version.

That night we arrived in Turin. We slept at an inn. I dropped from fatigue, but as my father undressed me I asked:

"And Giandouia. . . ?"

"That's for tomorrow night," said my father as he tucked me in, "because tonight he's as tired as you are."

For the first time I went to sleep without saying my evening prayers.

The next day my father took me to see Giandouia. I had still never been to the theater. I was in heaven during the whole show, missing not a single gesture of the numerous life-size marionettes moving on the stage. But I understood nothing of the plot, which, as far as I remember, must have been set partly in the Orient. When it was all over, I couldn't believe it. My father told me:

"The marionettes won't come back."

"Where did they go?" I asked, checking to make sure that Maldino was still in my arms.

My father made no reply.

Afterward, I left for Paris with my uncle. I never saw my parents again. They died a few years after I left.

▪

Having finished his story, Giovanni Moroni stared off for a long time. I tried at several points to have him tell me his memories, his impressions of the years since his earliest childhood. But it was impossible to draw him out on this subject. Anyway, I think he had nothing to say. . . .

THE FAVORITE

TO JOSEPH BACHÈS

It was in Beausoleil, near the Monacan border, in that part of Carnier called Tonkin and inhabited almost exclusively by Piedmontese.

An invisible executioner bloodied the afternoon. Two men were bearing a stretcher, sweating and breathing hard. From time to time they turned toward the sun's slit throat and cursed it, their eyes almost closed.

Those men and that stretcher plodded along like a scorpion fleeing danger, and, when they stopped near a low and filthy shack, the one on the back end slumped over, so the scorpion seemed to be on the verge of killing itself with its own tail. The rear bearer pulled aside the cover and exposed the wounded head of a dead man.

Through the open door of a house filled with men came a monotonous voice calling out the numbers drawn for Lotto. Crouched in the doorway, a thirteen- or fourteen-year-old girl, in rags, her short hair gnawed away by alopecia, repeated endlessly these words of starvation, humming them: *la polenta molla, la polenta molla. . . .* The bearers knocked at the door and at the shack's only window, calling:

"Cichina! Hey! La Cichina!"

Immediately an unkempt worker knocked the singing girl aside and came out of the house with the Lotto numbers flying around in it:

"What is it?"

Mopping their brows, the bearers replied:

"The rock he was drilling came loose. He fell a hundred yards down to the road, and got all torn up by the cactus."

The shanty door opened and La Cichina, that is to say Françoise, appeared, clean, with a pink apron, starched and escalloped.

She had dark hair, was still beautiful and well built. She was smiling insincerely and affectedly, and her skin, dry and dull as corn straw, alone attested that she was nearing her fifties. The shadows of her years ran along her neck and face. And in her eyes, still moist as the velvet of an otter swimming on the water's surface, the hard shivers of regret and an end of hope set from time to time the cold blue glistening of steel.

The impetuous passions of this working-class woman did not come across as any emotion. She felt this, and did her best, by the mobility of her mouth, her eyes, by dramatic gestures, to show the violence of her feelings, which she did not obey, naturally.

Her attitudes were noble, but studied.

She said: "He's dead!" And with a loud cry hid her face in her apron and there was nothing in her grief that did not seem faked. Quickly she lowered her apron and turned to the man standing in front of the Lotto house:

"Today's the third, Constantzing! . . . He died on the third! Bet on three, Constantzing, bet on three!"

A crowd was forming around the stretcher. There were little boys who sounded like men. There were little girls with babies in their arms. There were several workmen who started playing Odds and Evens right in front of the dead man.

A well-dressed gentleman stopped near the stretcher.

La Cichina looked at him and simpered and snivelled:

"He was so brave, so brave! I'll have a beautiful crown made for him."

The bearers picked up the stretcher again and carried it into La Cichina's shack. The dead man entered nonchalantly, like an oriental potentate. He was set down in the middle of the one room, which smelled of incense, sour pasta, and the stench of smoked dry cod soaking in a basin of glazed earthenware, placed on the ground. At the far end of the room was the bed; above it a rosary, hung on the wall beneath a woven palm branch, framed a lithograph depicting Victor Emmanuel between Garibaldi and Cavour.

The well-dressed gentleman had come forward; commiseratingly he looked at the pathetic interior of the mortuary house. La Cichina looked at him again and simpered:

"Meesta," she said, corrupting the word *mister*, "he's dead! He's dead! I have no luck. . . . But I see that a gallant gentleman like you does not take me for a woman of no account: poverty, meesta, forces me to live with misfortune and the unfortunate. . . . And who knows? Maybe we are going to win some money. He died on the third and Constantzing took that number in Lotto. Ah, yes! I too have been lucky. . . . When you're beautiful! . . . No one was more beautiful than I at Pinéreul."

And she burst into sobs, speaking of Pignerol, hiccoughing broken and magnificent sentences in which *il re galantuomo*, this Victor Emmanuel, who is the Henry IV of Italy, suddenly came back to life with his big conquering moustaches, his popular tastes, and his one-day favorites.

"*Vittorio Emmanuele!* . . . Yes, *meesta*. During a trip to Pinéreul. . . . He was the first, I swear it. . . . I had four *marenghi*, yes, meesta, four gold coins. . . . He was so handsome and he was the king. . . . Four *marenghi*. . . ."

And she wept, this favorite, letting herself go, abruptly letting all her years crumple her face. Her memory had called them all back, her own years and older ones which, aging her even more, evoked the gallant adventures of the prisoners once at Pignerol. It was Lauzun, frivolous old shade who came back to court this woman, and with superintendent Fouquet and the Man in the Iron Mask, formed a marvelous and secular court for this dead worker to whom chance had given as companion a king's favorite.

But Constantzing, who had lost his money at Lotto, chased these shadows away when he returned. He came forward, his fists clenched:

"You know, La Cichina belongs to me! Just because you're all dressed up doesn't mean you can stick your nose into other people's business. . . . So take a walk and *ciao!*"

And he repeated several times the hard Piedmontese goodbye: "Ciao! . . . Ciao! . . ." But La Cichina put her hands on her hips:

"Go on, silly, Constantzing, get out of here! You're surely not jealous of him?"

She pointed to the lithograph depicting Victor Emmanuel.

"Or of him?"

She gestured toward the dead man in the middle of the room.

"Well, you have no need to be jealous of the meesta here who is interested in me. I do what I want, you hear me, you bum, what I want! . . . I had a king when I wanted and masons when it pleased me and gentlemen, if I liked. . . ."

And Constantzing was a *botcha*, that is, a day-laborer, red-headed and strong, barely twenty and prouder of his Cichina than she was proud of her own fate. Jealousy came out of him the way foam comes out of a wave broken against a rock.

He flung himself on his mistress, who, stumbling over the stretcher, knocked it over and fell on top of the dead man.

Savagely, this king's rival stomped on the favorite on top of the cadaver, while glaring defiantly at the sovereign portrait hung on the wall.

THE DEPARTURE OF THE SHADOW

TO MADEMOISELLE SEGRÉ

It was more than ten years ago, and it isn't completely in the past, since I see, when I wish, the things and people of that time. I feel their substance and I hear the sounds and voices. These memories pester me, like flies you wave away and which immediately land again on your face or hands.

When Louise Ancelette died I was no longer in love with her. For the past year her tenderness had slid off me like water off a duck's back. My disaffection, which I didn't want to show, suddenly shone forth, in a labial flash, in front of our friends, to whom my misgivings gave, I'm sure, a subject for conversations which I guessed at without actually hearing, as, without seeing it, you intuit a young girl's cadaver when you walk past a house where someone has died, with its door decorated with white hangings.

Later I was told. Nearly a month before Louise's passing, I was saying she was going to die, that she had no more than three weeks left, then two weeks, then that she'd go next Wednesday, then that she'd die the next day. It was taken as joking, because Louise was in good health, youthful and gay.

But the butcher can tell on which day the heifer will be slaughtered. My hate was wise, I knew the very day she would die and she died on the day I had predicted.

She died suddenly. To the doctors her death made perfect sense, but

I couldn't stop my friends from suspecting me of a crime. Their questions wound around me like hissing snakes that I didn't know how to charm.

Old torments, I can still feel you. . . .

▪

A month before Louise's death we had gone out together. It was a Saturday. We wandered silently through the Marais, and, I remember, I watched our shadows ahead of us, overlapping.

In the rue des Francs-Bourgeois we stopped in front of a shop on which could be read: *Pawn Shop Merchandise*. Through the windows all kinds of objects could be seen on display. The entire world and all periods were the suppliers for that shop where jewels, dresses, paintings, bronzes, trinkets, and books were side by side, like dead people in a cemetery. I was sadly reading this lamentable summary of civil history formed by all these curios, when Louise asked me to buy her a jewel she liked. We went in. Opening the door I read the name written on its panes in white letters: "David Bakar," and I saw that our shadows, suddenly separated, came in only after we had.

▪

David Bakar was sitting at his counter. He told us to take the jewel from the window, and, after bargaining, when I was ready to pay, he told us he had no change and that I should go next door for it. I understood that this man didn't want to work on the sabbath, and when I came back and paid what I owed, the money stayed on the counter.

"What a beautiful day," David Bakar said to us then. "It's true that today is Saturday: the sun always shines on Saturday. And it's the best day for examining a shadow. And every Saturday reminds me of one of the most moving moments in my long life. The wonderful memory of having been chance itself! The Christians have no such memories of childhood.

"I was born in Rome and didn't come to Paris until I was 25.

"You know that in Rome the Lotto drawing is every Saturday, on the Piazza Ripetta, and that the job of drawing the numbers at random falls to a Jewish boy who is chosen preferably for his pleasing face and curly hair.

"Once, it was I who drew Lotto. My mother, who was very beautiful, took me. And so, in the middle of the square, I became chance. And since then I have never seen so many anxious faces looking at me.

When it was over there were eyes flaming with anger and others with joy. Men shook their fists and insulted me while others exulted and called me Jesus, Easter Lamb, savior, or other names flattering to a Christian.

"And I remember very clearly one man, in a frock coat and hatless, in the front row of the crowd. He seemed overwhelmed with sadness, and, as the crowd was dispersing, I saw that in the sun this man had no shadow. Quickly and discreetly he took a revolver out of his pocket and fired a shot into his mouth.

"Horrified, for a moment I watched the people carry his body away. Then I looked for my mother, but I didn't find her and I went back home alone. She didn't come back that night.

"When she came home the next day my father scolded her as we felt she should be scolded, my sisters and I. But he stopped short when she said a few harsh words which I didn't understand.

"My uncle Penso, the rabbi, came by that evening. He was irritated with my parents for their having let me draw Lotto. 'I saw David,' he said, 'he was like the golden calf which our masters worshipped in Moses' absence. I was waiting for the winners to organize a dance around David.' And his objurgations were mixed with citations from Maimonides and the Talmud."

▪

I offered Bakar a cigar which he refused, pleading the Sabbath.

▪

"Oy," said Bakar, "I don't feel very well. Before you go, lend me your shadows. . . . I want to know if I have long to live. I know a little sciomancy, or shadow divination. I learned the principles of this science from that same uncle who didn't like the golden calf to be worshipped, but who, extremely rich and miserly, traveled only in third class. One day one of his friends asked him the reason for this stinginess. 'Because there is no fourth,' replied my uncle. Soon after, he emigrated to Germany, where the trains do have fourth-class cars.

"Let's go outside, and, in the Sabbath sun, let us be sciomancers.

"You do have your shadows, don't you?

"Because don't forget that according to our true beliefs the shadow leaves the body thirty days before it dies."

▪

Outside the shop we happily saw that we still possessed our shadows. Bakar placed us in such a way that our shadows mixed with his. Then he examined that quavering shape. He said:

"Oy, the sign of fire! Oy, fire, *asch!* Oy, Adonai! *Asch* which is fire in Hebrew gives *Aschen* in German. That's ashes, the ashes of the dead. Oy, and hashish is from that, most likely. That will be a sound sleep. Oy, the sign of fire. *Asch, Aschen,* hashish, and assassin, which I forgot, all come from that. Oy, oy! Asch, aschen, hashish, assassin, oy, Adonai, Adonai!"

▪

And since he had come outside without a hat and perhaps as confirmation of a fatal foreboding symbolized by *asch*, the sign of fire, Bakar sneezed loudly:

"Achoo! Achoo!"

Deeply moved, I said:

"God bless you!"

But Bakar went back into his shop, saying:

"I still have a long time to live."

Then, seeing that the sun was going to disappear, he said to us:

"Another time."

Because it was time for his prayer. And, walking away, we could see him, wearing an old top hat and standing in the shop doorway as he read from a Hebrew book, which, as is proper, he started at the end.

▪

We were walking along without talking, and, after a while, when I felt the desire to see our shadows again, I saw with a singularly atrocious pleasure that Louise's had left her.

THE POSTHUMOUS FIANCE

TO LOUIS CHADOURNE

A young Russian who was traveling on the Continent went to Cannes for the winter. He boarded at a professor's, who, during the season, gave French lessons to foreigners.

This professor, around fifty years old, was named Nutmeg. He was a man of simple ways, and would have gone unnoticed had he not always reeked of garlic.

Mme. Nutmeg was a soft creature, who, thirty-eight to forty years old, looked no more than thirty or thirty-two. She was blond, with skin in full bloom, slender, but with wonderful curves in the hips and breasts. However, she was in no way provocative and she seemed sad.

The young Russian noticed her and thought her pretty.

The Nutmegs lived in a small white villa on the Suquet side, with a view of the sea, the Lérins Islands, and the long sandy beaches where troops of slender, naked children frolic in the summer, before dusk. The villa had a garden planted with mimosas, irises, roses, and big eucalyptus trees.

The Nutmegs' boarder passed the entire winter strolling, smoking, and reading. He didn't see the pretty girls the town is filled with, nor did he look at the beautiful foreigners. His eyes retained only the dazzle of the mica which sparkles everywhere, on the sea sand, on the streets, and on the walls; and his thought, when he walked against the sea wind, was all of Mme. Nutmeg. But this love was sweet and exquisite, not feverish, and one he dare not confess.

The eucalyptus trees carpeted the ground with small, odiferous hairs. There were so many of them that, dimming the mica's shine, they completely covered the gardens' paths, and the mimosas ignited all their scented flowers.

One evening, in the penumbra of a room whose window was open, the young man saw Mme. Nutmeg light a lamp. She moved slowly; her silhouette seemed a gracious and nonchalant vision. He thought, "Let's not postpone this any longer." And, approaching her, he said:

"What a pretty name, Mme. Nutmeg. It's almost a first name. It suits you whose hair is like a little sunlight in the east. You who are aromatic like the most heavenly scented nutmeg: when swallowed by a pigeon and rendered intact. Everything that smells good smells like you. And you must have the taste of everything that is delectable. I love you, Mme. Nutmeg!"

Mme. Nutmeg showed no emotion, neither anger nor gladness, and after glancing out the window, she left the room.

The young man remained completely disconcerted for a moment. Then he felt like laughing, lit a cigarette, and left.

Toward five o'clock he came back and saw M. and Mme. Nutmeg leaning against the garden gate. When they noticed him they came out into the street, which was always deserted. Mme. Nutmeg closed the gate and went over next to her husband, who spoke.

"Sir, I have something to say to you."

"In the street?" asked the young man.

And he looked at Mme. Nutmeg, who, placid, didn't flinch.

"Yes, in the street," affirmed M. Nutmeg.

And he began:

"Sir, be good enough to listen to my story until the end, our story, since it is Mme. Nutmeg's also.

"I'm fifty-three years old, sir, and Mme. Nutmeg is forty. It was twenty-three years ago today that we were engaged, my wife and I.

She was a dance teacher's daughter. I was an orphan, but my situation provided enough for a household. It was a marriage of love, sir.

"You see her now pretty and still desirable. But if you had seen her then, sir, with her hair in braids the hue of which cannot be found in any painting! Everything fades, sir, and her hair now, I swear, gives no idea of what it was when she was seventeen. It was honey. Or, one would have hesitated to say whether it went better with the moon or the sun.

"I adored her, sir. And I dare say she loved me too. We were married. It was an infinite joy, an exultation of our senses, a dreamlike happiness, a dream without disillusion. Our affairs prospered, and our love endured.

"After a few years, sir, it pleased God to fill the cup of our happiness even further. Mme. Nutmeg made me the father of an adorable little girl whom we named Theodorine, because God had given her to us. Mme. Nutmeg wanted to nurse her, and, would you believe it, sir, I became even happier to love that admirable wet-nurse of an angelic baby. Ah, what a charming picture, when, in the evening, beneath the lamp, after having suckled the little child, Mme. Nutmeg undressed her. Our mouths met often on the soft, smooth, sweet-smelling body of the little one, and our joyous kisses smacked on her little behind, her little legs, her dimpled little thighs, all over, all over. And we found adorable words: little devil, apple of my eye, weasel, ermine, and so many others!

"Then there was the first step, the first word, and then, alas, sir, she died at the age of five.

"I still see her on her little bed, dead and beautiful as a little martyr. I still see the little coffin. She was taken from us, sir, and we lost all our joy, all our happiness, which we will find again only in heaven, where our Theodorine goes on living.

"From the day of her death our souls felt old and there was nothing left in life for us to love. Still, we don't want to lose it. Our existence became sad, but it is so calm that it is delicious for that.

"The years have passed, attenuating the always persistent grief which makes us cry when we speak of our daughter.

"We often said about her:

"—She would be twelve now, this would be the year of her first communion.

"And that time we cried all day on her grave in our fragrant cemetery.

"—Today she would have been fifteen and perhaps would have been proposed to.

"It was I who said that, two years ago. My wife smiled sadly and we had the same idea. The next day we put up a sign: *Room to rent for single gentleman*. And we had several young people as tenants, some English, a Dane, a Roumanian. And we thought:

"—She would be sixteen. Who knows? Perhaps our tenant would appeal to her?"

"Then you came, sir, and we often thought:

"—Theodorine would be seventeen and surely, if she had not already married, her heart would choose this mild young man, well bred and in every respect worthy of her.

"You are moved, sir, I see that. You have a good heart. . . ."

"Alas, I was wrong. You see, sir, what you wanted to do this afternoon was almost a crime. Because the truth is, sir, Mme. Nutmeg told me everything. You have grieved the heart of this exquisite woman. You grieve my soul, sir, and you understand that after what has happened you may never enter my home again. See, the gate is closed, and it's over; you will never walk through my garden again. You thought it a garden of forbidden delight, sir, and that thought drove you out. You would not want to go back into this quiet house where you have saddened this woman who already loved you, I know, as a mother loves her son. Alas! I would have wanted to see you in my house for a much greater time, but, you feel it, you are convinced, it's impossible, it's over. Tonight you'll find lodging in a hotel and you'll tell me where you're staying. I'll send you your baggage. Goodbye, sir. Come, Mme. Nutmeg, night is falling. Goodbye, sir, be happy, goodbye!"

THE BLUE EYE

TO LOUIS DUMUR

I love to hear old ladies talk about when they were little girls.

▪

"I was twelve years old and I was boarded in a convent in the Midi of France," recounted one of these respectable ladies who have such good memories. "We lived there, cut off from the world, and only our parents were allowed to visit us, once a month.

"Even our vacations were spent in that convent surrounded by immense gardens, an orchard, and vineyards. . . .

"I can say that I left that enclosure of calmness only in order to be married, at the age of nineteen, and I had been there since I was eight. I still remember it: when I had crossed the threshold of the large door that opened onto the universe, the spectacle of life, the air I breathed and which seemed so new to me, and the sun that seemed brighter than it had ever been, freedom finally seized me by the throat. I was suffocating and would have fallen, dazzled and numb, had not my father, who was holding my arm, held me up and then led me over to a bench which happened to be there and where I sat down for a moment to recover my wits.

▪

"So at twelve I was a mischievous and innocent little girl and all my companions were like me.

"Studies, prayer, and devotional exercises took up our time.

"Nevertheless it was about that time that the demon of coquettishness penetrated the class I was in, and I haven't forgotten the trick he used to teach us that the little girls we were would soon become young girls.

"Not one man was allowed inside the convent premises, except the venerable chaplain who said Mass and preached, and to whom we confessed our peccadillos. There were also three old gardeners, not much to give us any great idea of the stronger sex. Also our fathers came to see us, and those of us who had brothers spoke of them as if they were supernatural beings.

"One evening, at nightfall, we were returning from chapel and walking in single file, heading toward the dormitory.

"Suddenly in the distance, behind the walls that surrounded the convent gardens, the sound of a horn was heard. I remember it as if it happened yesterday: the heroic and melancholy fanfare burst forth in the deep silence, at dusk, while every little girl's heart beat harder than ever. And that fanfare, reflected back by echoes, died out in the distance, evoking for us I don't know what fabulous cortege. . . .

"That night we dreamed of them. . . .

▪

"The next day a little blond girl named Clémence de Pambré, after leaving the classroom for a moment, returned completely pale and whispered to her neighbor, Louise de Pressec, that in the dark hall she had encountered a blue eye. And soon the entire class knew of the existence of the blue eye.

"We no longer listened to the Mother who was teaching us history. Presently the students were giving ridiculous answers, and I, who wasn't very strong in that area, when I was asked whom Francis the First had succeeded, made a wild half-hearted guess, that it was Charlemagne, and my neighbor, charged with brightening my ignorance, was of the opinion that he had succeeded Louis XIV. There was something other than the French royal chronology to think about: the blue eye.

▪

"And in less than a week, each of us had the occasion to encounter it, that blue eye.

"We were blind to the facts, that's for sure, but we all saw it. It passed quickly, making a beautiful azure splash in the darkness of the hallway. We were terrified by it but none of us dared mention it to the nuns.

"We ransacked our heads trying to figure out to whom that frightful blue eye belonged. I no longer know which of us put forth the opinion that it must be the eye of one of the hunters who had passed by a few evenings before, among the sounding horns whose lyrical blasts were enough to make you cry and which persisted in our memories. And so it was decided.

"We all persuaded ourselves that one of the hunters had hidden in the convent and that the blue eye was his. We never imagined that the single eye indicated a one-eyed man, or that eyes do not fly along the corridors of old convents, or wander about detached from their bodies.

"And nevertheless we thought of nothing but that blue eye and the hunter it evoked.

"We were no longer afraid of the blue eye. On the contrary, we wanted it to stop and look at us and we made it so that we often had to go out in the halls alone, to encounter the marvelous eye which from then on had us under its spell.

▪

"Soon coquettishness got mixed in. None of us would have wanted to be seen by the blue eye with our hands spotted with ink. Each did her best to look her best when going down the halls.

"There was neither looking glass nor mirror in the convent, but our own natural ingenuity soon made up for that. Every time one of us passed a door with panes on a landing, a section of black apron flattened behind the pane formed an improvised mirror, where quick, quick you'd look at yourself, arrange your hair, and wonder if you were pretty.

▪

"The story of the blue eye lasted for a good two months: then it was encountered less and less, and finally one thought of it only rarely, and when it was mentioned now and then it was never without a shudder.

"But in that shudder there was some fear and also something which resembled pleasure, the secret pleasure of speaking of a forbidden thing."

▪

You have never seen the blue eye go by, O little girls of today!

THE DEIFIED INVALID

TO DOCTOR PALAZZOLI

One spring morning, on the road from Paris to Cherbourg, a car exploded in the commune of Chatou, at the edge of le Vésinet. The two travelers in the coupe were killed. As for the chauffeur, he was picked up half dead; he was unconscious for several months; and when, in a little wheelchair pushed by his wife, he was finally able to leave the hospital, he was missing his left leg, left arm, left eye, and he had become deaf in the left ear.

From then on he lived in a cottage he owned by the sea, near Toulon. His insurance had left him relatively free of money problems. Because the surgical scars left by the cutting of his limbs were still painful, it had been impossible for him to bear a wooden leg or an artificial arm, and he had become, in a few weeks, accustomed to hopping instead of walking.

▪

The neighbors and passersby cast curious glances at this invalid who, while walking, seemed to be skipping rope, and that sort of dance communicated to his intelligence such a liveliness that his mind, with its felicity of repartee and subtlety of witticism, very quickly became well known far and wide. People came to see him and ask him things, not only from Toulon but from all the surrounding villages, and they soon understood that this man, named Justin Couchot—who was soon nicknamed The Eternal—had, along with much of the left side of his body, completely lost the idea of time.

▪

The two months he had spent unconscious had removed from him any memory of his life before the accident from which he had emerged disabled, and if he had partly recovered his use of the language he heard around him, it was now impossible for him to connect the various events which were from now on to fill his existence. He no longer understood the succession of his jerky acts.

To tell the truth, it seems impossible to believe that they appeared simultaneous to him, and the only word which, in thinking of men accustomed to the idea of time, can describe what was happening in Justin Couchot's brain is "eternity." His actions, his gestures, the impressions which struck his only eye and only ear, these seemed eternal to him, and his solitary limbs were powerless to create for him, among the various actions of life, that connection which two legs, two arms, two eyes, and two ears make in the minds of normal men and from which results the idea of time.

Strange infirmity that deserved to be called divine!

▪

His popularity grew each day, and he became used to exciting public curiosity. When the weather was nice, he went leaping along, flinging himself toward the heavens, where God is placed, and to whom he bore a mental resemblance, and immediately fell back to earth, a powerless god trapped in a body so weak and disabled that it inspired pity.

And if he were called upon for questioning, he stopped and stayed for hours perched on his leg like a stilt-bird.

▪

They asked him:

"Hey, Eternal, what did you do yesterday?"

He answered:

"Children, I create life. I wish that there be light and the darkness stays close by, but yesterday is not for me, nor is tomorrow, and nothing exists but today."

And he fit so well into nature that nature was for him an effect of his will, to which events responded endlessly, before he could know regret or desire.

A beautiful young woman simpered one day:

"Eternal, what do you think of me?"

"Million beings that you are, of all shapes, and with so many faces: child, young girl, woman, and old woman, you live and are dead, you are laughing and you are crying, you love and you hate, and you are nothing and you are everything."

A political man wanted to know which party he favored.

"All," answered The Eternal, "and none, because they are like light and shadow and must live together, with no possibility of change."

It happened that he was told the story of Napoleon.

"Good old Bonaparte!" exclaimed Justin Couchot. "He never stops winning battles, being defeated, and dying at St. Helena."

And as someone, astonished, asked him about death, he went hopping off, saying:

"Words! Words! How can you die? One is, that's enough. One is like the wind, the rain, the snow, Napoleon, Alexander, the sea, the trees, the towns, the rivers, the mountains."

The whole world and all of time were thus for him a well-tuned instrument which his one hand played perfectly.

▪

Justin Couchot disappeared a year ago and no one has ever known what became of him. The authorities, not without reason, assumed he had drowned, but his weird body with single limbs was never found. His relatives, neighbors, and those who had met him do not believe The Eternal is dead and they never will.

SAINT ADORATA

TO FERDINAND MOLINA

I once visited the little church of Szebeny, in Hungary, and I was showed a highly venerated shrine.

"It contains," the guide told me, "the body of Saint Adorata. It was almost sixty years ago that her tomb was discovered, quite nearby. No doubt she was martyred in the early days of Christianity, during the Roman occupation, when the Szebeny region was evangelized by the deacon Marcellin, who was present at the crucifixion of Saint Peter.

"In all likelihood, Saint Adorata was converted by the deacon's voice, and after her martyrdom, some Roman priests buried her blessed body. It is supposed that Adorata was simply the Latin transcription of her pagan name, because it is thought she received no baptism other than in blood. Such a name does not elicit Christian thoughts; however, the well-preserved body, which was found intact after so many centuries underground, rather showed that she was one of the elect, who, among the host of virgins, sing the holy glory in heaven. And now it's been ten years since she was canonized in Rome."

I listened vaguely to these explanations. Saint Adorata was not of extraordinary interest to me, and I was going to leave the church when my attention was drawn by a deep sigh which died away next to me. The person who had exhaled it was a smartly dressed little old man who was leaning on a cane with a coral pommel and staring at the shrine.

▪

I left the church and the little old man left behind me. I turned around to take one more look at his elegant and old-fashioned silhouette. He smiled at me. I greeted him.

"Do you believe, sir, the explanation the sacristan gave you?" he finally asked me, in French with the rolling Hungarian r's.

"Goodness!" I replied. "I have no opinion on these religious questions."

He continued:

"You are just passing through, sir, and it's been such a long time now I've wanted to reveal the truth of all that to someone, so now I want to tell it to you, on the condition that you will tell no one in this country."

My curiosity was aroused and I promised what he wanted.

"Well, sir," the little old man said, "Saint Adorata was my mistress."

I drew back, thinking I was dealing with a madman.

My astonishment made him smile, while he said to me in a lightly trembling voice:

"I am not crazy, sir, and I told you the truth. Saint Adorata was my mistress!

"I'm telling you, if she had wanted I would have married her! . . .

"I was nineteen when I met her. Today I'm over eighty and I have never loved any woman but her.

"I was the son of a rich castellan outside of Szebeny. I was studying medicine. And very strenuous work had exhausted me to the point that the doctors advised me to rest and to travel for a change of atmosphere.

"I went to Italy. It was in Pisa that I met her, and I immediately gave my life to her. She followed me to Rome, to Naples. It was a trip in which the sites were made more beautiful by love. . . . We traveled up to Genoa and I was thinking of bringing her here, when one morning I found her dead beside me. . . ."

▪

The old man interrupted his story for a moment.

When he resumed, his voice quavered more than before and I could hardly hear it.

▪

"I succeeded in hiding my mistress's demise from the hotel people, but only by resorting to the tricks of a murderer. And when I think of all that, I still shudder. No one suspected me of a crime and they believed that my companion had left very early that morning.

"I'll spare you the details of the dreadful hours spent next to the body, which I had put in a trunk. In short, I was so clever that the embalming went unnoticed. The coming and going, the great number of travelers in a large hotel gives them a relative freedom and impersonality which were very useful to me under the circumstances.

"Then there was the trip and the problems raised by Customs, which I was able, thank heaven, to get through. It's a miraculous story, sir! . . . And by the time I got back home, I had become thin, pale, unrecognizable.

"Going through Vienna, I had bought, from an antique dealer, a stone sarcophagus which came from I no longer know which famous collection. At home I was allowed to do what I wanted, without any worry about my schemes, and no one was surprised by the weight or the amount of baggage I had brought back from Italy.

"I myself cut the inscription ADORATA and a cross on the sarcophagus, in which I enclosed, wound in wrappings, the body of the woman I adored. . . .

"One night, with an insane effort, I moved my love to a nearby field, so I could find the location only I knew about. And, alone, I came to that spot to pray every day.

▪

"A year went by. . . . One day I had to leave for Budapest. . . . Imagine my despair when I returned, after two years, to see that a factory had risen on the very spot where I had buried the treasure that I loved more than my own life! . . .

"I almost went crazy and thought about killing myself, when that evening, the parish priest, during a visit, told me how, when they were digging up the nearby field for the factory's foundations, they had found the sarcophagus of a Christian martyr from the Roman era, named Adorata, and that they had moved that precious reliquary to the modest village church.

"At first I started to explain it to the priest. But I changed my mind, thinking that in the church I would be able to see my treasure whenever I wanted.

"My love told me that my beloved was not unworthy of the religious honors being given her. And today I still believe her worthy of them, because of her great beauty, her unique grace, and the deep love which perhaps caused her to die. Besides, she was good, mild, and pious, and if she weren't dead I would have married her.

"I let things take their course and my love grew into devotion.

"She whom I had loved so much was declared venerable. Later she was beatified, and, fifty years after the discovery of her body, she was canonized. I went to Rome myself to be present at the ceremony, which was the most beautiful spectacle I have ever been given to look upon.

"With that canonization, my love entered heaven. I was happy as an angel in paradise, and I quickly came back here, filled with the most sublime and strange happiness in the world, to pray at the altar of Saint Adorata . . ."

▪

Tears in his eyes, the smartly dressed little old man went away, tapping the ground with his cane with the coral pommel and repeating:

"Saint Adorata! . . . Saint Adorata!"

THE TALKING MEMORIES

TO MAURICE RAYNAL

When I was in London I took a room in a boarding house that had been recommended to me and where I was given a comfortable room where I slept quite well.

▪

The next day I was awakened early by the sound of a conversation taking place in the room next door.

I understood quite well what was being said, in American English spoken with the soft Western accent. The dialogue was between a man and a woman, a passionate conversation.

"Olly, why leave me without warning me? Why? Why?"

"Why, Chislam, because my love for you would have interfered with my freedom, which means more to me than love."

"So, blonde Olly, you loved me and that love was the reason I lost you?"

"Yes, Chislam, I would have ended up giving in to your entreaties and I would have married you. But in doing so I would have given up my art."

"Wild Olly, I'll wait for you forever."

And the dialogue continued in that vein: the independent Olly refusing to accept proposals of marriage from the amorous Chislam.

What I knew of Anglo-Saxon prudery made me wonder at first

why a lady visitor was permitted next door, then I thought no more about it.

▪

My astonishment increased when, the following morning, I was awakened by a new conversation. This exchange was taking place in French, but with the accent typical of Americans from the West.

Chislam was again talking with a woman.

"You don't love me anymore, Monsieur Chislam! You're always around Olly, the little dog trainer, who's as thin as a rail. It was just a month ago you fell into ecstacy when I sang my love song, and it was love that made you feel that way, because I don't have much of a voice."

"I finally noticed that, Miss Criquette. Besides, you don't love me. You are making fun of me with your flirting."

"So, you've forgotten your promise of marriage and that country house in a village on the Loire where we were supposed to spend our honeymoon?"

"Miss Criquette, I decided that if I married, I would retire in Maine, but the Maine in the United States."

"And so you're right. Go ahead, Monsieur Chislam, because I wouldn't have married you with your mug, your mug, your mug! . . ."

Other remarks followed, and while getting dressed I thought: "This French girl has a funny accent. She must have lived in California for quite a while. . . . God, how crazy she is about this word 'mug' and how fickle this Chislam is! But this boarding house is, after all, not one you'd recommend."

▪

The next day I was rudely awakened, as I had been the day before. This time the exchange took place in Italian and still with the deplorable accent of the American West.

"Beautiful Locatelli, yield to my love. Let's get married! We'll give up traveling and go hide our happiness in a villa I'll buy in California, in San Diego. I want a view of the wonderful bay and we'll grow oranges."

"It's impossible, Signor Chislam. I'm engaged to one of my countrymen who is an officer in Bologna. He has only his pay and we're waiting until I have enough dowry for us to get married."

"So, goodbye, Signorina Locatelli. A poor clown like me has no hope of winning your heart from a brilliant officer. Goodbye, signorina. And so that you can be happy as soon as possible, allow me to complete the dowry you mentioned."

I thought: "This singular Lothario is a nice man. Still, his mania for a daily marriage is quite inconvenient: it wakes me with a start, and much earlier than I'm used to getting up."

▪

But the following night I didn't sleep a wink.

Mr. Chislam was talking with a man, in the new English of the United States and with the Western accent.

"Yes, Chislam, you're just a poor guy who'll die alone, with no family, loveless."

"You're right, Chislam, and I must resign myself to it. In my lifetime I've entertained millions of people all over the world and I haven't found a wife."

"Chislam, you've been a universal joy, the very laughter of the entire world. It was too much for one woman. What is for everyone might, by its enormity, frighten an individual."

"So, Chislam, I who thought of myself as the funniest of men am in fact the unhappiest!"

"Alas, Chislam, I agree with you! Your fantasy, which unleashed in everyone a joy unexpected until then wasn't enough to make an ordinary girl love you. Lost in the crowd, she could laugh with it. But if, face to face, you spoke of love, you inspired only an infinite sadness!"

"So that's the way it goes, Chislam?"

"Chislam, that's the way it goes!"

"And now I have no one left to console me, Chislam, except myself."

"No one, except yourself, Chislam."

This melancholy dialogue between the mysterious Chislams would presumably have lasted a lot longer, if, at the end of my rope, I had not beat loudly on the partition between us, yelling:

"Gentlemen, it's getting late. Time to go to sleep!"

Immediately the two Chislams fell silent and I soon sank into a deep sleep.

▪

But, around eight o'clock, how great was my stupefaction when, rudely awakened, I heard that my neighbor had resumed his matrimonial banter with the independent Olly, the first woman whose voice I had heard.

I got dressed as quickly as possible and went to find the respectable hostess of the boarding house.

"It's impossible for me to sleep in the room you gave me. My neighbor talks with women who come to visit him as soon as day breaks and with men at night."

"You're a light sleeper, sir. You'll be given another room, on another floor.

"Your neighbor is an estimable man.

"He's the famous comedian Chislam Borrow. He was born in California and his tricks, his faces, his ventriloquism act, and quick-changes allowed him to do one-man shows, which made him famous all over the world. He is highly educated and he knows several languages.

"Then, age came with success. Chislam Borrow is now an old bachelor. He has neither friends nor relatives. He's been lodging here for three years now, and speaks to no one, except himself. His ventriloquism gives him a way to have company when he feels like it.

"Often he gets into a conversation with one of the women he would have wanted to marry. Sometimes he talks to himself, and these are the saddest conversations.

"Chislam Borrow is to be pitied, sir, because, you know as well as I, these talking memories are not, despite their variety, worth the simple talk of a wife whose hair would have turned white along with his, this disconsolate, retired comedian—and who would now console him in his old age. . . ."

Some time thereafter I left London without having seen Chislam Borrow.

THE MEETING AT THE MIXED CLUB

TO DOCTOR CHAPEYRON

After having earned a rather large fortune in the mines of Colombia, the Dutch engineer Van der Vissen left for Paris, which he had visited in his youth. Having spent more than twenty of his forty-five years in South America, he saw Paris as the place to have a good time.

Van der Vissen was a large man, blond, strong, quarrelsome, a gambler, and completely lacking in scruples. Being established in Paris had been the goal of his life. He thought that the pleasures to be found there were superior to those offered to voluptuaries at all other points on the globe.

▪

The day after his arrival, the Dutch engineer ran into a former worker from Panama, who, dressed like a gentleman, looked like someone who was doing quite well. If he himself had not made a fortune, he was to be found where they are unmade, for he had become a tout for a big gambling club, a mixed club which was open every night, near the Trocadéro. Convincing Van der Vissen to go there was easy. Drawn by his passion for gambling and for women, the Dutchman, who kept his entire fortune in his wallet, in bank notes, went one evening to the club.

The formalities having been expedited by the club's management, Van der Vissen entered the gaming hall, which was in full swing. He started playing, and, with luck backing his boldness, he won at first in an ostentatious streak. Then he took the bank, and when his luck changed all of a sudden, he had the worst possible run. When he yielded his spot the bad luck followed him, and the more he lost the more he insisted on betting heavily. The bank notes melted in his hands like snow. Then, when he was cleaned out, he did his best not to show it, and it was with a smile that he mopped his brow.

▪

Near him stood a dark-haired young woman, tall and lithe, with dark circles under her eyes, highly affected, elegant, and loaded with jewels. Van der Vissen watched her. She was playing wildly and winning like mad.

The beauty of this woman and her extraordinary luck made a strong impression on the Dutchman's mind. Since he was a fellow gambler and persisted in looking at her, the beautiful woman smiled at him.

Van der Vissen wanted her with his entire being, her and her jewels and the winnings she would carry away. His adventurer's instincts were aroused. He now felt for this woman, her gold, and her jewelry a mad passion which had to be satisfied.

The adventurer's life prolongs one's youth, and Van der Vissen did not look at all old. With a primitive and completely awkward gallantry, and with emphatic words, he attracted the young woman and offered to see her home.

She replied in a languorous voice whose inflections enflamed the Dutchman's passion even more.

And, mixing praise with promises, he made it so that finally they left together.

▪

She lived in the rue de la Pompe, in an elegant apartment where, when they were inside and the lights turned on, Van der Vissen asked about the help: but the maid was asleep in her room upstairs.

▪

They were now in a boudoir furnished with divans large and low, and with hassocks strewn with gloves, letters, packages of Egyptian cigarettes, and books of modern verse.

Like a crazed gambler who, for the first time, decides to cheat, Van der Vissen hesitated a moment as to what he was about to do.

Then, as the young woman was raising her arms to take off her hat in front of the mirror, he hurled himself on her and tried to grab her throat. But she whirled about and gave him a really manly punch in the nose. At the same time a male voice, totally unlike the one affected until then, crudely insulted the engineer in the grossest and lowest terms.

He was dealing with a solidly built young man, who could, by putting on airs appropriate to his shameful condition, ape the frailness of a waif, but who, when it came to fighting, was someone to contend with.

And Van der Vissen still wanted this being, whatever it was.

Desperately, since he had nothing left to lose and had revealed his scheme, he desperately wanted to have at least the last word in this adventure. And a frightful pleasure came over him as they were tearing at each other. . . .

▪

There were cries, and gun shots were heard. And, the next day, these strange enemies were found dead next to each other, as if death alone could be the criminal child of a passion so brutal, of such a sterile love.

LITTLE RECIPES FROM MODERN MAGIC

TO JEAN MOLLET

The following manuscript was found in front of the omnibus office on the Place Pereire, the tenth of July this year.

I'm holding it at the owner's disposal if he can give me its exact description.

I have no idea of the real value of the recipes you're about to read. But they seemed to me sufficiently odd to arouse one's curiosity.

The magician's industry, which in our time is taking on the proportions of one of the most enjoyable arts—I'd almost say one of the most useful to high society—magic, had to undergo numerous transformations to get out of the ruts laid down by charlatanism and routine. The abuse seen in this last century, with table-turning, all kinds of mediums, hypnotism, cards, offhand palmistry, coffee grounds often harmful to the health, as in Turkey, for example, have given birth to troublesome and often exaggerated prejudices. The magician has been replaced by the fortune teller, if not by the clairvoyant.

But since the magician, refusing to compete with these absurd rivals, calls for surprising combinations from science and the fine arts, concerns himself above all with hygiene, studies the raw materials, arranges them in a rational manner, since finally magic has taken on new forms in perfect harmony with good taste and reason, these prejudices have greatly diminished. They will disappear completely when creations made for the theatre and costume parties are distinguished from those destined for good company. For the former, the recipes for fast results, but too violent to endure. For the salons, the simple and suave combinations, the serious methods, which, without appearing to do so, master destiny, and which, in short, confer power and talent.

Considered from this double point of view, the magician's art merits the esteem and the interest of sensible people. I hope to show one proof of this in these recipes chosen for use by society people.

Salve for avoiding car trouble

It's very easy to make. You take several fillets of sole—new shoes are not necessary, old ones being fine for this use: in fact the sole should be aged well. Take every precaution that the sole not take on your odor as you clean it—to do so, dredge your hands in flour beforehand. Cut the sole into pieces and put them in a basket in the oven. When they have lost all their moisture, grind them up in a mortar and pass the dust through a very fine sieve. Finally, mix it with a solution of horse fat. You'll be delighted with it.

Poetry meters

It sometimes happens that such-and-such a young man—nearly a child—becomes highly successful in the salons with his metrics or with others' metrics, and one would wish to do the same.

Go to work for the gas company and you'll learn all about meters; if the recipe doesn't succeed, go to a gymnasium and learn about isometrics; and if that fails, study the metric system.

Another recipe for poetry

You should always carry an umbrella you never open. Revealed by M. André B., this recipe is supposed to have been entrusted to him by our dear M. P.F., prince of poets.

N.B. This most effective recipe is not easily used.

Vinegar for pennies from heaven

Take three pounds of freshly picked ice leaves. Peel them and spread them to dry somewhat; do not forget to stir from time to time so they won't warm up. Next let them marinate in twelve quarts of good Orléans vinegar. Then distill in a double boiler, over a medium heat at the start. You will easily obtain eight quarts from this operation and pennies will rain down in abundance.

Antihygienic powder for having lots of children

Powdered beans from last season	3 kg
Sifted sugar	1 kg
Magnesium	11 cc

Season it all with dried rose petals. Sprinkle it on your bedsheets and do not get up until you have succeeded.

Eau de vie for speaking well

Para cress (spilanthus oleiacenus) in flower and with stems removed	125 g
Alcohol at 33 degrees	500 g
Macaroni	10 g

Shake well before using, then wash your feet thoroughly with it.

Incantation for beating the stock market

Every morning you will eat a red herring while uttering forty times before and after: "Bucks and plug, clink and drink." And after ten days your dead stock will become live stock.

Recipe for glory

Carry with you four fountain pens, drink clear water, have a great man's mirror, and often look at yourself in it without smiling.

Remedy for arthritis

Drink gin and water and you'll see its effects before two months.

END OF THE LITTLE METHOD

▪

It should be added that trustworthy people, among whom M. René Dalize, have used some of these recipes and have acknowledged their complete effectiveness.

THE EAGLE HUNT

TO PAUL LOMBARD

I had been in Vienna, in Austria, for a week. The rain never stopped falling, but the weather was mild, although it was midwinter.

I was bent on visiting Schonbrun, and, deeply moved by it, walked about the damp and melancholy park where this tragic King of Rome, fallen to the level of the Duke of Reichstadt, had wandered.

From the height of the Gloriette, whose name—ironic diminutive—must have made him think of his father's glory and of France, I looked down at the Hapsburg capital for a long time, and, with night, when the lights came on, I set off toward my hotel, located in the middle of town.

▪

I got lost in the suburbs, and, after numerous detours, I came to a deserted street, wide and poorly lit. I noticed a shop, and although it was quite dark and seemed to be not in use, I started to go inside to ask the way, when my attention was drawn to a passerby who brushed past me. He was short, and an officer's cape fluttered on his shoulders. I picked up my pace and caught up with him. I saw him from the side, and when I made out his features I reeled back. Instead of a human face, the being standing next to me had the curved beak of an eagle, solid, terrifying, and infinitely majestic.

▪

Overcoming my fright, I started walking again, closely examining the strange character with a human body topped with the head of a bird of prey. He turned to face me, and, as his eyes bore in on me, a quavering old man's voice said, in German, some words the meaning of which were:

"Don't be afraid, sir, I'm not bad. I'm very unhappy."

Alas, no response was forthcoming, no sound emerged from my throat, dry with anxiety. The voice continued, but imperious and tinged with scorn:

"My mask scares you. My real face would scare you even more. No Austrian could look on it without terror, because, I know, I look exactly like my grandfather. . . ."

▪

At that moment a crowd invaded the street, running and shouting. Others came out of the shops and faces stared out of the windows. I stopped and looked behind me. I saw that the people coming were soldiers, officers dressed in white, liveried lackies, and a gigantic Swiss mercenary who was brandishing a long cane with a silver pommel. A few stableboys were running around them carrying flaming torches. I wondered what could be the object of their chase and I shifted my gaze to see where they were headed. But the only thing I saw in front of me was the fantastic silhouette of the man in the mask with the eagle's beak, as he fled, his arms spread and his head turned as if he wanted to measure the danger menacing him.

And, in that instant, I had a precise and particularly moving vision.

Seen thus from behind, his elbows spreading his cape and his beak in profile above the right shoulder, the fugitive formed a perfect image of the heraldic eagle that furnishes the coat of arms of the French Empire. This glorious prodigy appeared for barely a second; nevertheless, I understood that I had not been the only dupe of an optical illusion. The eagle hunters stopped, abashed by its look, but their hesitation lasted only as long as the apparition.

▪

However, the poor bird-man turned his beak away and then all we had before us was some unfortunate man making a desperate effort to escape his implacable enemies. They soon caught up with him. In the glimmering light of the torches, I saw their sacrilegious hands swooping down on the trapped Eagle. He cried out things that struck me with panic and paralyzed me to the point that it didn't even occur to me to rush to his aid.

His supreme cry meant:

"Help! I'm the heir of the Bonapartes. . . . "

▪

But the blows fell on his beak and silenced his outcry. He fell lifeless, and those who had knocked him down picked him up quickly and ran off with his body. The crowd disappeared around a corner. I tried to catch up, but it was hopeless, and for a long time I stood at the corner of the street they had taken, watching the shifting glimmers of their torches disappearing. . . .

▪

A short time after that extraordinary encounter, I went to a party given by an Austrian lord whom I had known in Paris. There were wonderfully beautiful women there, many diplomats and officers. I found myself for a moment with the master of the house, who said to me:

"A strange but persistent rumor is now going around Vienna. The newspapers don't mention it, because it is too obviously absurd to find credence among people with any sense. Still, it could be of interest to a Frenchman and that's why I want to let you know about it. It is claimed that a secret marriage would have brought together the Duke of Reichstadt and a young lady of our high nobility, and that a son of that union would have been reared without the knowledge of even the court insiders. That illustrious personage, the authentic heir to Napoleon Bonaparte, would thus have lived to an advanced age, and, if one were to believe the rumors going around, he would have died barely two or three days ago, under particularly tragic circumstances, the exact details of which we don't know. . . ."

I said nothing, not knowing what to say. And, at that fashionable party, I recalled the painful apparition of the old Eagle who had spoken to me, and who, wearing on his face masked by State order the superb sign of an august race, perhaps was the son of the Eaglet.

ARTHUR, THE ONCE AND FUTURE KING

TO BLAISE CENDRARS

On January 4, 2105, there was seen in the streets of London a Marvelous Knight of Sparkling and Magnificent Bronze. The passersby thought, "What is this masquerade?" And when they saw him, women of all classes shivered right down to the roots of their hair, whispering, "What a handsome trooper!" because they took him for some showman.

The handsome stranger headed for Buckingham Palace. At the gate the mounted guards started to bar his way, but the champion, with a single glance their way, inspired their respect, and they let him pass.

At the palace door he was asked:

"Who are you?"

He replied:

"The Knight of Papegaut."

"What do you want?"

"The Adventure of this Castle."

At that moment the king's daughter, informed of the Marvelous Knight's coming by one of her retinue, came to the window and almost fainted at the sight of the paladin. The follower had to support her mistress and pat her hands. The princess, regaining her composure, looked again at the Bronze Knight, and couldn't believe her eyes.

Suddenly she broke free, thin and light as a butterfly, and went to find the king. George IX—in England called "Branny," because his face was covered with freckles, as though he had been dipped in a sack of bran, and in French-speaking countries called "Le Breneux," in a detestable play on the English word "bran"—was told by his daughter of the arrival of the Marvelous Knight of Sparkling and Magnificent Bronze. The king smiled, saying that it was no doubt some prestidigitator looking to put on a show at the castle and who did not require his personal attention. But the princess insisted that her father have the knight brought up.

To please his daughter, George IX gave in. He rang and ordered the jester to be led in.

The Knight of Papegaut was brought to the king, who was seated in a nice old armchair, his legs crossed.

Seeing him, George IX, dazzled, stood up and asked:

"Are you not the jester?"

The Knight of Papegaut replied in a ruffled tone:

"I am your king."

George IX put up his fists, but his daughter the princess, chest thrust out, one fist on her hip, came toward the Knight, saying:

"And I will be the queen."

George cried out:

"Get the anarchist!"

At that command, officers, chamberlains, pages, and varlets came running from all directions. Among them was an old valet who was very wise and who had read as many tales of chivalry as Don Quixote. This old man, seeing the Knight, could not refrain from crying out:

"Is it Arthur?

"The once and future king."

And the latter said gravely, clasping the princess chastely to his breast:

"I am Arthur, your king, son of Igerne, brother of Uter Pandragon, and I once held court at Camelot. I am resuscitated, and for the past few days I have walked to get here, showing myself only to peasants, who took me for an apparition and from whom, in this short time and thanks to my natural gifts, I learned to express myself in your language."

If Arthur said nothing of his wife Guinevere, it was mainly because he was a widower and happened to have a new fiancée in his arms. And then also because that queen had cuckolded him.

George called a page, who, having listened to his master, hastened away. A few moments later a doctor and a goldsmith were brought into the hall. George IX took them aside and spoke to them under his breath. The doctor, who looked like Mr. J.cqu.s C.p. . . in the role of Thomas Pollock Nageoire, and the goldsmith, whose face recalled that of Mr. F.l.x. F.n..n, then approached the Bronze Knight and greeted him. The paladin smiled, took off his armor, and allowed the curious doctor to study different parts of his vigorous body, while the goldsmith examined the metalwork on the armor. The doctor was the first to turn to George IX, and, after exhausting the standard formalities, said to him:

"Sire, this gentleman is certainly of an origin older than one could possibly imagine. I would not even be surprised if he told me he had been born before Sesostris. His flesh is older than the oldest elephant hide, several hundred years old. A mammoth-steak frozen in the eternal ice of northern Siberia could hardly be compared, for all its healthy old age, with these miraculous buttocks."

And, so saying, he patted the Knight's behind.

The goldsmith was less explicit:

"Obviously," he said, "these arms appear to be of the period, but I should add that I myself have manufactured this type, which are displayed with honor in several well-known museums. However, if this gentleman is as old as the doctor claims he is, there's no reason why the arms can't be equally old."

But at this moment there came an answer to a telegram which the page had sent, on order from George IX. The latter, having read the telegram in a whisper, uttered these words:

"This telegram removes all my doubts. Here is its purport: *Arthur tomb empty.*"

He kneeled down and said:

"Sire, I return to you your realm and wish only to be the most loyal of your subjects. You shower me with honor in making my daughter the queen."

"Speaking of which," said Arthur, raising the dethroned king, "I will begin by getting married."

And while those present shouted, "Hurrah! Long life to King Arthur! Long life to the queen!" heralds ran through London announcing the news to the people.

George IX's abdication was soon known throughout the world. Meanwhile, Arthur was married and had a delicious wedding night.

On waking, after innumerable and indescribable revels, Arthur had a tailor come in to measure him for modern clothes. As is supposed, there was no coronation at Westminster Abbey, since Arthur had been king for centuries. The only services held, in the kingdom's Catholic churches, were funeral, as is proper, for the soul of the deceased queen Guinevere and for Lohok, Arthur's son sired with the beautiful maiden Lisanoz before he married the queen. This Lohok had a rather unfortunate life. He had attempted the adventure of the castle of the Douloureuse-Garde and failed, as had many other knights. He was rescued by Lancelot and died from an illness contracted in the castle prison.

The following days were spent by King Arthur listening to the kingdom's historians, who gave a brief account of what had happened since his death, and life resumed its ordinary course this very year of 1914, on April 1st, when I am writing this chronicle, George V reigning in England, and M. Raymond Poincaré presiding over the Third French Republic, while Paul Fort, prince of poets, is visiting his people in the most far-flung reaches of Scythia, and while, stretched out on a divan in the living room where I am, my friend André Billy is snoring artfully.

OUR FRIEND MÉRITARTE

TO JOSÉ THÉRY

Our friend Méritarte, who saw in man an artistic animal, was striving to create a culinary art which could not only satisfy one's appetite and gourmandise, but also address itself to the intelligence, as the other arts do.

It was nearly two years ago, in his little dining room overlooking the courtyard, sixth floor, rue Nollet, that we four savored the touching spectacle of the first edible drama.

▪

The hors d'oeuvres, composed of Vire chitterlings and filleted smoked herring, had a sinister look which made our hearts sink as it aroused our appetites, and the funereal lentil soup which then appeared made us worry as to how this strange party would end. We feared a dramatic turn of events. It happened in the form of a Rouennaise duck whose bleeding shreds, which the devouring guests fought for, had the expected dramatic effect. And when, after a lugubrious Rachel salad, composed of the yellowest potatoes and the blackest truffles, our friend Méritarte had, with a determined look, upset us with the explosions from a great many bottles of champagne, the feeling was at its height. And since there was neither cheese nor dessert of any kind, but only a little lukewarm coffee with no sugar, we left in a state of malaise hard to describe, and the impression left by that first culinary drama will never fade from our memories.

Some time after this somber tragedy, our friend Méritarte invited us to a comedy banquet. First there was a chilled soup madrilène which provoked smiles. But everyone burst out laughing when our host informed us of the taurine origin of the *criadillas* which followed. The pleasantries increased at a pretty fair rate around a calf's head whose buffoonery pleased us so much that we left only the parsley it had been trimmed with. An extremely rare leg of lamb was no less popular, with the garlic that gave it its aroma and the Soissons beans on which it softly rested appearing to be highly comical features. In short, we split our sides laughing, and the nice little white wine Méritarte poured for us encouraged our gaiety.

▪

But our friend Méritarte wanted to raise his art to lyrical heights. One evening he served us a vermicelli soup, soft-boiled eggs, a lettuce salad with nasturtiums, and cream cheese. We said that this was sentimental poetry, and, irritated, our friend Méritarte asserted that he would raise himself to the tone of the ode. It's true that a month later he served us a cassoulet in which his art finally attained the sublime. He even tried the epic, with a bouillabaisse whose Mediterranean flavor immediately reminded us of the works of Homer.

▪

But we were really surprised when our friend Méritarte announced to us that henceforth he was devoting himself to philosophy and that he was inviting us to become his disciples that following Thursday. We were right on time, but by our worried expressions it was easy to see that the metaphysics of the kitchen range inspired little confidence in us. We were right, because set before us was a plate of beef bones whose marrow was difficult to extract; there were also some rabbit heads which we had to crack open in order to suck out the brains; as for dessert, we had almonds, nuts, and, since it was Kings' Day, a cake whose bean did not serve to name a monarch, but evoked simply the wisdom of Pythagoras, at the end of this philosophical banquet.

We feared that, disillusioned, our friend Méritarte had taken refuge in a kind of devotion, which could have allowed him to serve us mystical meals. We were wrong: Méritarte, who had risen to the height of the epic, descended to the novel and ended by marrying his cook, who was a pretty girl. Having abandoned her stove, the new Mme. Méritarte, who didn't adjust to having nothing to do anymore, began to deceive her husband too much. For a while he seemed to have renounced his art. But, one day, he decided to give a big satirical dinner, to which he invited only his wife's lovers.

▪

Aside from Méritarte and his wife, there were a dozen of us there. The meal was as dramatic as possible: funereal soup, bleeding meats, etc. Mushrooms were served, and, for some reason, I didn't eat any. The platter was heaped with them and everyone treated himself, except for me, who left them on my plate. And thanked myself for it, because, at the end of the meal the guests, including our friend Méritarte, turned pale, complained of horrible pains, and died during the night, poisoned by toxic mushrooms.

▪

Thus, our friend Méritarte's satire truly reached its goal and killed those who were its object, including himself, who was tired of living and believed that he had exhausted the resources of his art.

▪

As for me, I've often tried to initiate cooks into this sublime cuisine which our friend Méritarte had discovered, but they just haven't understood. It'll be a long time, I thought, before the artistic endeavors of this man of genius will be resumed. Still, every domain of this new art has not been explored, and, for my part, I have always been surprised by the idea that our friend Méritarte never tried anything in the historical genre. It's true that he was by no means a scholar or scientist, but above all a man of imagination, a poet with a special gift for satire.

THE CASE OF THE MASKED CORPORAL, THAT IS, THE POET RESUSCITATED

TO THE MEMORY OF ANDRÉ DUPONT

The new Lazarus shook himself like a wet dog and left the cemetery. It was three o'clock in the afternoon and bills relating to the mobilization were being posted everywhere.

HERE'S
THE COF
F I N
IN WHICH
HE LAY
P A L E
A N D
R O T
T I N
G

He claimed a duplicate of his military papers at the police station, and, being in the auxiliary, had himself transferred into the armed services.

▪

He had been living for about three months at the depot of the Nth Field Artillery Regiment in N.m.s.

One evening, toward six o'clock, he was gloomily reading this curious notice which decorates a bare wall on a little street near the Arenas:

PLATO AND COMPANY

HAS NO BRANCHES

when in front of him arose a singular corporal whose face was covered with a blind mask.

"Follow me," the strange mask said to him. "And watch the rum deals! . . . Warning!"

"I'm following you, corporal," said the new Lazarus, "but, tell me, are you wounded?"

"I have a mask, gunner," said the mysterious corporal, "and this mask conceals everything you'd like to know, everything you'd like to see, it occults the answer to all your questions since you've come back to life, it strikes dumb all the prophecies, and thanks to it, it is no longer possible for you to know the truth."

▪

And the resuscitated gunner followed the masked corporal. They came to the Carmes church and took the Uzès road that led to the barracks.

They entered, crossed the honor yard, and went behind the buildings up to the park, where, having leaned against the left wheel of a 75, the corporal suddenly took off his mask and the resuscitated poet saw before him all he wanted to know, all he wanted to see.

In great landscapes of snow and blood he saw the hard life at the Front; the splendor of exploding shells; the awakened look of exhausted sentries; orderlies giving the wounded something to drink; the sergeant, liason officer to an infantry colonel, impatiently awaiting his girlfriend's letter; the platoon commander taking the watch in the night covered with snow; the Moon King floating above the trenches and crying out not in German but in French:

"It is for me to remove from him the crown I gave to his grandfather."

At the same time he was throwing little bombs filled with anguish and madness on his Bavarian regiments; in the Garibaldi Corps, Giovanni Moroni was taking a round in the belly and dying thinking of his mother Attilia; in Paris, David Bakar was knitting balaclavas for the soldiers and reading *L'Echo de Paris*; Viersélin Tigoboth, riding the near horse, was driving a Belgian gun and limber towards Ypres; Mme. Nutmeg was caring for the wounded in a hospital in Cannes; the fonipoit Paponat was assistant to quartermaster-sergeant in an infantry depot in Lisieux; René Dalize was commanding a machine-gun company; the bird of Benin was camouflaging pieces of heavy artillery; at Szebeny, in Hungary, an elegant little old man was committing suicide at the altar where the remains of Saint Adorata are at rest; in Vienna, Count Polaski, whose castle is on the outskirts of Krakow, was haggling with a second-hand dealer over a singular mask in the shape of an eagle's beak; *feldwebel* Hannes Irlbeck was ordering his recruits to slaughter an old priest from the Ardennes and four defenseless girls; the old ventriloquist Chislam Borrow was on his way to performances in the hospitals of London, to entertain the wounded. And the shells were bursting in marvelous sprays.

Then the resuscitated poet saw the deep seas, the floating mines, the submarines, the fearful flotillas. He saw the battlefields of eastern Prussia, of Poland, the quiet of a little Siberian town, fighting in Africa, Anzac, and Sedul-Bar, Salonika, the stripped and terrible oceanic elegance of the trenches in Barren Champagne, the wounded second-lieutenant carried to the ambulance, baseball players in Connecticut, and battles, battles; but at the moment he was about to see the end of all this and what he wanted to know above all else, the corporal put his blind mask back on, and, before leaving, said:

"Gunner, you've missed roll-call. You are reported absent."

And at that moment the bugle sounded the tender, the melancholy call of taps.

Before getting back to his barracks, the resuscitated poet, looking upward, saw that in the sky the stars had been arranged, and, without dimming, were shedding their sweet-smelling petals; points of impact of millions of cries from earth and sky, they were forming this bright inscription:

LONG LIVE FRANCE!

▪

he sleeps in his
little soldier's
bed my resuscitated
p o
e t

Then he left like the others with a detachment. . . .

▪

And the Front lit up, the hexahedrons were rolling, the steel flowers were blossoming out, the barbed wire was growing thinner with bloody desires, the trenches were opening like females before males.

While the poet was listening to the shells miaowing above the hypogea soldiers dig out, a marvelous Lady was caressing her necklace of attentive men, this unequalled necklace, a panethnic river streaming with innumerable lights.

And the frieze horses were foaming in the rain.

O glaucous day where the regiment of sites goes.

O trenches, deep sisters of the walls.

Come by horse as far as the front lines, with a firewood-gathering party, and enveloped by asphyxiating fumes, the corporal in the blind mask was smiling amorously at the future, when a fragment of a high caliber shell hit him in the head, from which sprang, like pure blood, a triumphant Minerva.

Stand up, everybody, to give a courteous welcome to victory!

Design by David Bullen
Typeset in Mergenthaler Optima
and Granjon by Wilsted & Taylor
Printed by Maple-Vail
on acid-free paper